tigerLily

tigerLily

BOOK | **TWO**
PineLight Series

JILLIAN PEERY

First Ebook Edition: May, 2012
First Paperback Edition: May, 2012
Ebook ISBN: 978-0-9837507-9-6
Paperback ISBN: 978-0-9837507-8-9

To book a signing event, submit your request at
www.jillianpeery.com.

First Paperback Edition
Printed in the United States of America

For my family.

I am a message in a bottle
tossed carelessly into the deep blue sea.

My future is unknown.

PREFACE

WHISPERS FLEW IN THE AIR OF THE CASTLE HALL, WHIPPING around like a confused whirlwind. The heavy chains jingled around my wrists as I stepped to the podium. All seven senators paraded around in long white robes, none daring to look at me directly. Maybe they recognized the traits of my father in me—maybe the same shaped eyes or the way that I stood tall under scrutiny. Maybe this unnerved them. Their strange sandals shuffled through the madness, their robes swished behind them.

The silence then was brittle, like I was standing on a frozen lake and any minute I would fall—any minute that frail ice would break, and a bitter, cold death would surround me.

I started to worry about them not looking at me.

Nervously, I shifted my weight on the makeshift podium, making the wooden structure creak. It was hard to keep a calm composure in their presence. I knew the penalty for my alleged crimes—death, and there was no way around it. I wasn't innocent by any means, but to be marked a traitor and judged as one seemed completely unfair. It was love that had been my crime, not treason. Perhaps they would issue my punishment quickly. Perhaps it would all be over soon. I told myself to breathe. That was all I could do now. *Just breathe.*

Finn stood tall, brave, holding my hand so gently in his. He knew, just as I, that what happened in the next few minutes would change both of our lives; yet he managed to keep an expressionless face. Until he spoke.

His strong voice captured the attention of every person in the crowded hall, though his statement was directed to the line of senators. I didn't need to hear his words to know what he was saying. His face told his story now. The lines of his lips curved down as each word left his mouth—his brows wrinkled with despair. I tried to stop him from speaking. I tried to prevent him from ruining everything, but my voice went unheard. Then it was too late. He had said too much.

This was the man that I loved with every part of my existence, and he was sacrificing everything he had to save me. My life was already on trial, but for him to surrender his was unbearable. As I stood awaiting the senators' verdict, I no longer worried about the outcome of my judgment day; I worried about his.

-1-

GRIEF

Dark waves broke against rock and sand at my feet, greeting me with a somber splash of hello. It was an appropriate greeting for tonight.

The neck of a slim bottle slipped back and forth between my loose fingers, sloshing the remainder of the red wine on my white shorts. It would stain, but I didn't care. Not tonight. I was searching for the perfect location for my ridiculous ceremony. The ocean was loud, but I could still sense the paper tapping against the second bottle, the one packed in my satchel—the one already sealed with a message.

By the time I reached the perfect spot, a spot that, only a year ago, led me to the hidden cave, the bottle in my hand was completely empty. I shoved a note through its circular glass lips and corked it shut. My mind felt fuzzy from the wine rushing through my veins, but I was still determined to do what I had set out to do. I had two bottles, with two messages. Each going out to someone I loved. My father. My Finn.

In my heart I knew they would never read a single word I had written. They would never feel what I was feeling as I rewrote each sentence over and over until it looked and sounded just right. But this was something I had to do. I had to try one last time.

I placed my feet on a large sturdy rock, quietly whispered my wish, and then I tossed both bottles into the moonlit sea. As I watched the grey waters engulf each bottle like a hungry soulless creature, I felt my hope swallowed up with them. All my hope was lost tonight, taken effortlessly by the ever-changing sea.

Day broke, bringing a new kind of sadness with it. Today was my father's funeral.

Inside, Scarlet Heights was silent and warm, intensely bright in spite of the depressing day. The hall where the long maroon rug stretched had welcomed many guests over the last few hours. Family friends came by the carloads to pay their respects to my father. Some knew of our family's history, but those who didn't questioned his disappearance—his death. The story that circulated through each room was a story of him being lost at sea. It was the only way to explain his missing body. I found it odd that so many bought into the lie.

I made my way through the sobbing mourners until I found an empty place to sit. Thankfully it was the single gold-cushioned sofa chair that was available. It was a perfect spot, secluded, wedged in the corner of the room, slightly hidden by the large curtain that was pulled open for the day.

Fergus led Norma through the sea of faces, stopping to greet each person, while my mother and Aunt Alice sat on a love seat across the room flipping through an old photo album. Mom's brow was crinkled, a sign that she wouldn't stay composed much longer.

I had cried myself to sleep the night before, letting the tears flow freely in the hope that my eyes would stay dry today. Even though loving and caring friends surrounded us, I still felt a strong need to hide my emotions—to hide my weakness. Fergus said that this was a trait of a guardian. It was a trait of his, at least, because in spite of all the sadness I knew he had seen, I had yet to see him cry, even once. But I could sense that he had to work hard to keep the tears away, just as I did.

My eyes watered. I quickly redirected my gaze to the wood-framed window beside me.

How strange it was that the day didn't share our sadness. The roses outside the glass window were in full bloom, the round bushes freshly shaped, and the grass was healthy and green. I could see the angel fountain in the center of the courtyard, running its steady stream of water, glistening from the sun. The bright scarlet hues surrounding the fountain gave the courtyard a Valentine's Day feel. A couple of birds floated through the crisp blue sky, adding to the effect. The day didn't feel right, not at all. I wanted it to be dark and gloomy with lots of rain. A monsoon would feel right. *If I could only make it rain,* I thought.

Lost in my thoughts, I missed the soft patter of feet parting the crowd behind me.

"De little nightingale sits and stares through rose-colored glass," said a deep Cajun voice.

"Maytide!"

"My eyes be happy seein' you, child."

5

She greeted me so differently than the others, throwing her arms around me without a bit of hesitation. The smell of Louisiana bayou radiated from the fabric of her colorful dress, taking me back to the life I had left to find this one. A white smile stretched across her face from one round cheek to the other.

"Oh dis is good! De child be surprised," she said, a chuckle escaping her dark lips and causing her stomach to jiggle against me.

"I didn't think I would see you again."

"Surely you didn't tink you'd rid of ol' Maytide dat easily?" She tightened her arms, giving me one last squeeze before releasing her grip. "Now, give me a twirl, so I can see dis dress dat you be wearin'!"

I gave a quick turn, allowing the black folds of fabric to sway at my knees. It was a nice dress, made with a lightweight silk and overlaid in lace. It was a dress that Norma had bought for me to wear today. I had added a few things of my own, of course—the heavy cross pendant of pine light that never left my neck, a wide belt around my waist, and sneakers that contradicted the entire outfit. No one seemed to mind.

"Oh! How fine!" She lightly touched the fabric on my shoulder, inspecting the small pattern in the lace. "Mighty fine."

Her aged hands pushed my hair behind my ear.

"I like de hair, too. It be shorter dan I remember," she said. "It suits you."

I was surprised that she liked the change. After an entire year, my hair had barely grown long enough to touch my collarbone, probably half the length it had been when I last saw her. A little self-conscious,

6

I raked my fingers through it, loosening the waves that had naturally formed throughout the morning.

"Thanks," I said, wondering if she really meant what she had said.

A voice broke through the room, pulling our gaze to a white-headed priest. All of the priests looked the same here. Same aged leather Bible in hand, same black clergy shirt and white clerical collar. Their voices were no different. Same Irish tone, same rhythmic diction.

"If everyone could follow me," he said, warmly, "we are about to start the ceremony outside."

No one said a word as we stepped out into the warmth of the day. We followed the priest out of the courtyard and sauntered through untamed golden waves of wheat to the location my mom had picked for the ceremony. It was a nice spot, just past the walls of Scarlet Heights, through the hairy field, but not too close to the wild forest beyond the grains. It was a perfect place, circled with warm sun, looking out over the ocean.

The priest spoke, but I could only hear my own thoughts ringing in my ears. The former glory of Scarlet Heights was still visible here. The manor, both innocent and beautiful, peaked above the stone walls built centuries ago for its protection. In a way, guardians were much like those walls. Our sole purpose was to protect the innocent—to protect this world from the purest forms of evil. I had been born in the lost world, a place that had no name, other than lost. A realm that God made just as he made the others, filled with both good and evil. But it was a dimension that held a darker kind of evil. And we, the guardians, were responsible to see that it never crossed through the gates. Our kind had been battling this ancient war since the beginning of time. Guardians, just like my family, were stationed all over the continent, always prepared for a battle we hoped to never fight.

Since my return from the lost world, there had been a change in me. At least, I saw something different when I looked in the mirror. My skin was the same cool shade of pale, spotted with the same freckles I'd known my whole life. My hair was the same auburn color, the same equal mix of natural red and brown. But I still saw something different. I didn't see the weak girl from the year before; I saw a woman. A strong woman.

I felt different, too. Sometimes I felt as though I could sense more change coming, like a cold coming on, or that dull pain you feel in your joints right before a storm. It was almost a natural growing pain, if that even made sense. My bones just sporadically ached. Fergus explained that there would be many changes as my ability formed, but he couldn't tell me what those changes would be. He didn't know. No one knew. But he kept saying that I was "at that age," whatever that meant. Until my gift decided to develop, I would just have to sit around and wait. I tried not to think too much about it, because I was nervous about what gift might come. I had already seen so many consumed by power and for power. I didn't want either to happen to me.

The priest cleared his throat, breaking my thoughts while simultaneously bringing me back to the ceremony.

I turned my focus back to him, watching the wrinkles on his face move as he talked. I still couldn't bring myself to tune in to what he was saying. I knew it would only bring the tears.

It was hard to let go.

Before, I couldn't remember what I'd lost, but now, I did. Now I remembered everything that made me love my father. His eyes, his smile, his rough Irish accent, the way he tried to protect me from anything and everything. The memories I had gained made saying goodbye even harder. It was bittersweet really. Finding those memories, only to be reminded of what I had lost. In solitude, I'd cried all over again, until there were no more tears. He had been a wonderful father. He had taught me everything I needed to know to survive in his world—in both worlds.

My eyes burned again.

Mom was a heartbreaking silhouette in black. She stood quietly looking out to the sea as the priest read from his open bible. Black lace covered her face, and tears silently escaped from underneath. Fergus stood by her, gently holding her hand in his. Norma was next to him, twisting a mascara-stained handkerchief that Maytide had passed to her.

After the service, the priest stood with Mom, offering more comfort with scripture, while Fergus and Norma made the rounds, thanking everyone for coming and inviting them to stay for food. I saw this as my opportunity to slip away from the crowd.

Feeling the tears stubbornly roll from the corners of my eyes, I stumbled my way down to the edge of the grassy platform. I sank down, folding my legs under me and allowed the tears to fall.

"No need for de cryin', child." I looked over my shoulder and noticed for the first time that Maytide had followed me. "Can I tell you somet'ing?"

I nodded, watching her slowly lower her round body so that it perched on a boulder that seemed out of place in the coppery land of grain. "What am I sayin'?" she muttered to herself. "Of course I can tell you somet'ing. Dis be somet'ing awfully good."

I sniffled a bit while I ran the back of my hand over my raw eyes.

"I don't think anything will sound good today."

"Oh no, child. You see," she leaned her whole body forward and lowered her voice to almost a whisper, "your father, he be alive."

I turned, stunned that she would say such a thing on a day like today.

"We can't live in that fantasy world anymore...we just can't." I looked up at her to catch her gaze. "All this time we have waited for a miracle...we have waited for my father to come home. But he's not coming back, Maytide. He's gone. I've come to terms with it—we all have. Don't you see my family needs this? We need closure."

"Dis be no fantasy, nightingale. He be alive just as you and I be sittin' here."

"What makes you believe he's still alive?"

"Because I see him. I see you both in my visions. You both fightin' de same war—both fightin' to stay alive, but you fight on different sides. I see him lost—just as lost as you were before."

"Visions?"

"Before you keep feedin' dat doubt of yours, know dat my visions ring true. Dat is dey gift given to ol' Maytide. My visions follow de order of de prophecy."

"Gift? Prophecy?" I questioned, not knowing which answer I was more curious about. "I thought you were a traiteuse? Are you saying that you are a guardian? And…and there's a prophecy?"

"People can be many tings, child. Defined in many ways. Just like you be guardian, you also be Irish and female. Brunette and pale. Gifted and chosen. Maytide be havin' many definitions." She stopped to chuckle. "I am no guardian, child. But you and I, we are from de same world. My people are de Zyons, and I am one of de few elders blessed with de gift."

"What? What gift?"

"You not be listenin' to me, child? It is de gift of prophecy dat I posses. I see tings—visions of de future."

"And you see my father? Alive?"

"Yes, dat is what I said."

"If you see him, then where is he? Why has he not come home?"

"De fallen, dey don't play fair. Dey play awful tricks on dey mind. Brainwashin' I call it." She rubbed her hands together as if she were getting ready for a fight. "I'd like to get my hands on one of dem evil-doers. Dat would be de day."

"Where is he?"

"I tink you know."

"I wouldn't be here if I knew, Maytide. Tell me where I can find him," I said. "Tell me how the prophecy affects us. Tell me why I've never heard of any of this."

I realized I was demanding a lot of answers, but if what she said was true, then I needed to know all of the truth.

"Dey don't talk of your father because dey do not see what Maytide sees. And dey won't speak of de prophecy because dey tink dey can protect you from it. But you must embrace it, child. You hold de key to a destiny far beyond your imagination."

"Tell me more about my father. About the prophecy. What are they protecting me from?" I asked. "Please, Maytide."

"I can tell you no more. I can't be interferin' with what be written."

Maytide wiggled her body forward on the rock until she was back on her feet.

"Maytide!" I scrambled to my feet to face her. "Please don't leave me to piece this together, to wonder if it's even true."

Her head shook. "I only give you what you need to hear. So hear dis, for I be sayin' it only dis one time."

Her eyes darted around, checking to see that we were completely alone before she spoke.

"Dere be a war in de makin'," she said. "In de end, someone will die and someone will live. Dat cannot be changed, but don't let your mind be your cage, little nightingale. Don't let it keep you from

12

what you truly want. Open your mind, awaken your gift."

"Who will die? My father? Finn? Is it me? Please—you have to tell me."

"You must find de answers yourself," she said, taking her first step away. "Awaken your gift and follow de tiger lily down. It is de only way."

"What? Maytide, wait..." I pleaded, but she had already turned her back to me. The fabric of her dress swished around her as she moved further and further away to join the scattering mourners.

A cold fear raced through every inch of me, as if an ice-cold bucket of water had been poured right over my head. *My father is alive?* And how could she tell me that someone was going to die? Who was going to die? Me? When would this happen? How could she give me so little information?

I had tried every possible way of getting back in the cave, but since my return to Ireland, the waters had risen to block its only entry. How could I help anyone if I couldn't get back to the lost world? I'd spent a year fighting the cold waters. It was impossible. And what did she mean by awaken my gift? A guardian's ability was something that had to develop in us, not the other way around. I had no control over when it would come.

After the mob of sad faces were out of sight, I started my walk back to the manor, alone. There were several cars that left Scarlet Heights, winding their way out of the long driveway, seeming like tiny blurs as I watched them from the distance. Close to three dozen cars remained parked along the square hedges, lined in perfectly even rows, with drivers napping as they waited for their passengers. Apparently, many of our guests chose to stay a little longer for the food.

When I got back through the gates, everyone had already gathered inside. Why had so many decided to stay? I wanted to be alone today. I wanted them all to leave so that I could cry for my father in peace. Or should I cry at all? Maybe there was truth in what Maytide had told me. Maybe my father was still alive. Either way, I wanted to be left alone.

As soon as my foot touched the first step on the porch, the tall doors swung open. An older gentleman stood politely behind them, waiting for me to enter. The same noisy buzz from before spilled out, nearly convincing me to stay outside, but my conscience insisted that I go in to check on my mother once more. I thanked the older man as I awkwardly continued past him. His strong aftershave made me wince, but I managed to hide my expression under a tight smile.

Luckily, many of the guests had already assembled in the grand dining hall, conversing over fancy china filled with homemade food. Only a few people were missing from the group, Mom and Norma being two of them.

The soles of my shoes tapped against the hardwood floor while I hurriedly passed each room, trying my best to go unnoticed. It was somewhat impolite to avoid the very people who were here to help us through all of this, I admitted to myself, but every sympathetic face only added to my depression.

I came to the end hall, finding both Mom and Norma facing the rosy glass panes. They stood shoulder to shoulder with their arms interlaced behind them, holding each other close. Norma's lips were moving, as she appeared to console my mother, but they paused to smile when I stepped into the hall. Apparently, I hadn't been invisible.

"Clara, my sweet girl. There you are," my mother said, turning to greet me. Her arms left Norma's and opened for a hug.

Nothing physical had changed about my mother. She was still the beautiful blonde from my childhood, with long hair full of curls and eyes of blue crystal. You could almost see her pure soul through those crystals. The only scars she'd received from her time in Hades were emotional.

Growing up, her sweet laugh was always in the air, a smile always on her face. She was happy, kind, and loving. Now, a mark of sadness was upon her. Written secretly on her face, heard in her subdued laugh. Only her love felt the same. It was hard to see her with tears streaming down her face, knowing that there was nothing I could say or do to make them stop.

My arms wrapped around her small waist, and my cheek fell against her shoulder. Her hands patted my back tenderly, as only mothers' hands can, bringing a moment of relief from the pain.

"Are you okay?" I asked loosening my grip. It was a dumb question to ask, one that I'd heard over and over from our guests, but I really wanted to hear that she was okay.

"I miss your father," she responded, lifting her hand to catch a stray tear. "It's hard to believe he's gone. I don't want to believe it."

"I know."

Norma stepped over to us, pulling us both in for an embrace. "Brogan was a good man," she said through a cracked voice. "The best son a mother could ask for. And he'd be proud to know that you are safe. That you both survived."

Norma kissed us both on the forehead, wiped her face with the same handkerchief she'd had since the ceremony, and forced another smile on her lips. She was trying her best to be a rock for the both of us.

"Now, Marie, I haven't seen you eat since yesterday. How about we all go get some food, hmm?"

Mom nodded.

"Clara, that means you too."

"You two go ahead. I'm not all that hungry." They both gave me a look, the look that meant they weren't convinced in the least. So I decided to tell them what they wanted to hear. "I'm going to step outside for some air, but I'll join you later. Save me some soda bread and colcannon, if there's any left."

My request seemed to work, bringing a quick grin to my mother's face. I stepped over to the round silver doors that were centered between the two rose-colored windows. A beautiful design wrapped around the edges of each door, swirling to meet with the handle. Every piece of Scarlet Heights was like this—intricate and beautiful. I opened one of the heavy doors just as Norma and Mom left the room.

The rushing sound of the trade winds comforted me now. Their cool, salty breeze pleased my warm skin. It was a sweet escape, but an escape that lasted only briefly before my mind took me back to a place of sadness.

My eyes trailed the path of green before me, leading to the gift, my cursed reminder of Edmund, a man that I'd learned to hate more and more with each day that passed. *Gift*. Ha!

The weathered statue still gazed over the water, just where he had left it. No one dared to move it for fear it had been cursed. So it sat there, day after day, week after week, a year since the day I'd almost died. Even marked with dark mold, the statue was as beautiful as the day it was given to me. It was much too beautiful to hate, even if it had been a gift from Edmund. *Gift*. Why did that word keep coming up?

Wait. Maytide had told me to awaken my gift. I'd assumed she meant my ability, but what if she meant the owl?

There was only one way to find out.

Before I had time to talk myself out of it, I was in arms' length of the frozen creature. My hand reached out slowly; my fingers trembled as they neared. My own subconscious encouraged me with every second, until my fingertips slid along the hard shape of the statue.

I expected the owl to break from the stone, to come alive and somehow transport me back to the lost world right then and there. But it didn't. When my hand moved along the cold stone, nothing really happened. No magic, no curse. Nothing.

Why had I thought this would work? I felt deflated with disappointment.

I had just turned toward the house, forcing my leaden feet to carry me, when a great *crack* like shattering glass broke the stillness. I spun back just in time to see the owl lift its wings, flapping its stone appearance away. Then it took flight. Of course, this was obviously something I hadn't planned for, much less anticipated. I'm not sure why, it was a bird, after all.

No, no, no. Don't fly away!

It hovered over the edge of the cliff for a moment, screeched, and then took off toward the field. I followed as quickly as my feet would carry me, blessing my own wisdom for wearing sneakers to the funeral. The owl led me on for almost a mile, past the earth that lined the edge of the cliff, around the random patches of red roses that colored the grounds of Scarlet Heights, through the tall golden grass of the field outside the gates, until I reached the edge of the woods that grew wild along the countryside. I had never crossed over into the forest. I was told it grew thick and that the territory was claimed by a pack of rabid wolves. That was enough to keep me out then, but now was different.

I stood for a moment, gawking at the sheer height of the aged trees, carefully eyeing the green woods for any sign of angry animals. The majestic bird flew further into the distance, leaving me no time to question my decision.

I stepped into the forest and didn't look back.

-2-

TIGER LILY

Bright green ferns hugged the trees, while thousands of clovers and flowering lavender English bluebells covered the ground. I noticed the owl would circle around a tree every so often, as if it were giving me time to catch up. I treaded on, almost another mile, stepping over decaying trees and puddles of water, skirting around prickly plants and heavy brush. I tried to step with a light foot, hoping to leave the forest undisturbed. A family of deer sprinted just ahead of me, darting deeper into the trees. My effort of silence was apparently a lost cause. But at least I hadn't disturbed any creatures of danger. No wolves, yet.

I stayed on a semi-straight path, following the owl as it swooped through the forest, until it finally decided to perch on a tree. Its wings fluttered and then folded into the fluff of its body as it dug its talons into a low branch.

Keeping my voice soft and gentle, I spoke to it while approaching the tree.

There were only a few steps between us when I tripped. My feet stumbled underneath me trying to find their way back to balance. But my legs wouldn't have it—my body met with the damp earth before I had time to react.

My toes stung inside my shoe, but I didn't notice the pain for long. There was something next to my foot, something more interesting than the throb in my toes. Sticking from the earth was the cause of my unexpected tumble: the corner of a stone. As I looked closer, I could see dozens of them, all half-buried, making a distinct line leading to the west of my initial path.

With a hushed flutter of wings, the owl breezed past me in the same direction as the path of stones.

"Wait!" I pleaded.

I hurriedly jumped to my feet and followed, being more careful where I stepped. The owl wound through the tops of the trees, flying over the path of the stones. Branches tore at my dress, but I pushed through them. I continued to call to the owl, hoping to compel it to stop. With the daylight already lessened to a muted glow, I wasn't sure how much longer I could chase him. Soon the entire forest would be overpowered with the night. I needed to turn back soon. I would have to, before the night released the wolves.

The forest was less dense ahead where the remainder of the daylight seemed to linger, so I decided to venture just a little further.

As I advanced, I saw the reason for this enduring light. Just beyond me, surrounded and protected by the roughness of the forest, was a small clearing. It was a circular area, no larger than my old bedroom in Coushatta. The entire circle was completely clear of trees and brush, with only a strange, vine-covered structure in its center. Ruins of some sort.

"Where have you brought me?" I questioned, as if the bird might actually reply.

The owl flew into the clearing and circled the pink sky until I arrived. As soon as I entered the circle, it landed on the highest point of the ruins, before swiftly transforming back into stone.

I stepped up to the ruins, letting my fingers glide over the vines as I stared up at the frozen creature. *What is this place? And more importantly, why did you bring me here?*

I parted the vines to get a better look at the structure. Underneath the layer of green was dark stone. It appeared to be marked with something, something like rust-colored paint or dried blood. I couldn't be certain.

My hands flew to work, pulling and ripping until all of the markings were unveiled.

This was definitely something. It had been no accident that the owl led me to this place. It couldn't have been. The markings were faded and even chipped in places, but there was still enough color to make out an image and a message.

The image was a very minimalist, almost childishly drawn picture of a person holding a long sword. I shifted my eyes to the markings below it, hoping that they might hold more meaning.

There were small spaces between each cluster. The Roman alphabet. Words. But it wasn't English. Over the last year, while I was homeschooled, my mother insisted that I learn the basics of Latin. I wasn't able to speak the language just yet, but I could read and write it for the most part. After a moment's study, I realized the curving, rust-colored script before me was definitely Latin.

> *De quorum sanguis regnum manet verum*
> *Etiam eget purus docebit electis per*

Of course! Latin was often used in the lost world, written on scrolls and painted on walls. If I remembered correctly, some of the elders even spoke the language. Did this mean that I'd finally found a link to that world? I let my brain go to work, piecing the message together. *Let's see...*Regnum *means "kingdom."* Sanguis *means "blood"...*I got it!

> *The realm awaits those whose blood runs true*
> *Only pure steel will guide the chosen through*

Though I could read the message, I still didn't understand. What was this blade of pure steel? And where was it? I focused back on the painting. The figure held a long sword shaped differently than any I'd seen. The pommel was unique in its kind, the blade engraved. *What does it say?* The painted words were simply too weathered with age.

I started to pace the length of the wall, biting my lip as I racked my brain. How was I ever going to find this sword? I knew nothing about it. There were swords back at the manor, hundreds of them, but none appeared special. None of the ones I'd seen, anyway. Fergus said they were just there in case the manor came under attack. Which was an odd idea in itself. I could never imagine an attack on Scarlet Heights, especially one that required swords. I couldn't picture the old world mixing with our modern world in Ireland.

Maybe the sword was around here. Somewhere in the forest. My eyes fell to the grass at the base of the wall, skimming the blades of green while I continued to think.

I followed the line of the wall and stopped when I rounded the corner. There were two sides to the wall, of course, and my answer lay on the other. Behind the crescent-shaped structure was a single orange flower, speckled with black. The flower was so bright, it pierced through all other colors scattered in the woods. Its bloom was like no other, brilliant with life and so unbelievably perfect in shape. It was a flower meant to be found. A flower waiting to be found. It was a tiger lily.

I rushed to the bloom, planting my knees firmly in the ground beside it. A small formation of grey stones circled it, separating the striking tiger lily from the wild vegetation of the clearing. Maytide had spoken of a tiger lily. Follow it, she had said.

I raked my fingers through the grass for a moment while I concentrated on her exact words. *Follow...the tiger lily...down...*

My heart palpitated as I shoved my fingers into the dark soil. I began to dig vigorously and with conviction as excitement pounded through me. The dirt was relatively soft at first, but after I had gone a couple of feet deep, it turned into hard clay. The roots grew deep—really deep, but I continued to shovel the clay with my bare hands.

I was completely covered in dirt and clay when I found the first root. I quickly wiped the sweat from my eyes, and then stood so that I hovered over the plant. With a firm grip around its stem, I pulled, hoping to free the remainder of the plant from the ground. It didn't budge. I repositioned my hands and pulled in the opposite direction. The earth around the roots buckled, but the flower was still in the ground. I leaned down further, placed my hands closer to the base of the stem, and gave it one last yank. The stem suddenly ripped from the ground, throwing dirt and clay into the air and sending me stumbling backwards.

I looked down into the hole that I had created, feeling pleased with my accomplishment. All of the dirt was now pushed aside, leaving only red clay at the bottom—and a glimmer of hope.

The hilt of a sword.

The pommel was a round silver ball, looped with small rings of gold and silver metal. This elaborate design carried through to the guard and grip of the sword with additional metal loops and curved bars. I slipped my fingers through the silver guard, tightened them around the hilt, and started to pull. Unlike the tiger lily, the blade of the sword slipped from the earth effortlessly.

The blade felt powerful in my hands, its steel beaming as it reflected the last shafts of sunlight. I quickly ran the bottom of my shirt over the steel, removing the remainder of clay to read the engraving.

"*Tantum purissimo tutorum limen transiero*," I muttered aloud. "Only the purest of guardians shall…pass."

This is it. This has to work, I thought, leaping from the mound of dirt I'd created and hurrying back to the wall.

I circled the crescent-shaped structure several times, removing the vines from the backside of the wall, just as I had on the front. After discovering no new markings, I moved to study the others.

I planted my feet before the wall, looking up at the message and image. Was my only clue a childlike painting of a figure in an archway holding a sword? *Well…it's worth a shot.*

My arms extended with the blade of Tiger Lily, as I'd decided to call it, keeping the tip pointed at the painting on the wall. I was careful when I walked forward, expecting to strike its hard surface.

But the resistance of steel against stone never came. Instead, I watched as the tip of the sword disappeared into the wall. Not an ounce of force was needed; the tip just vanished as if I'd stuck it through a sheet of dark water. I shifted back, pulling the sword out to check the steel. The blade was solid and felt cool when I ran my fingers over it. I pressed my hand against the wall, checking its rough surface.

I inserted the blade back into the wall, watching it disappear the same way as it had before. I pulled it out and examined it again. Still solid. Still cool. Was this really happening? After my year of searching, had I finally found a way back to the lost world? It was hard to fathom.

With all hope dependent on what lay ahead, I stepped forward, watching the blade disappear inch by inch until there was nothing left but the hilt and my hand wrapped around it. My heart knocked

against my chest. I took one more step forward, feeling a cool rush pass through me as I entered
darkness.

I had found my way back.

WATERFALL

My eyes met with blackness. A damp, musty smell in the air reminded me of mud pies and humid nights. Moisture beaded on my skin the moment I found myself in this stale, muddy darkness. The roar of rushing water was ahead of me. It was really loud, really close.

Once my eyes adjusted to the sudden darkness, I realized that I was standing behind a waterfall. Bats squeaked as they swarmed overhead before blasting through the wall of water about ten paces in front of me. Was this the only exit from this darkness? I looked back to see if the woods were still behind me, but all I saw was black rock. The gate had sealed.

I eased my way to the lip, squinting to make out what lay beyond the mouth of the waterfall. Ahead was a starry sky, and far, far below was dark water. That was all I could see around the steady stream. There was no way to properly judge the distance between where I stood and the lake of water below, but I had to hope it wasn't too far, and I had to hope it wasn't too shallow. It couldn't be, because jumping was my only option.

After stepping back a few yards and voicing a quick prayer, I slid the blade of Tiger Lily under my belt, positioning it against the fabric of my dress.

Once I felt it was secure, I sprinted to the edge, and then heaved my body into the falling stream.

The fall was further than I had anticipated. My mouth opened with a shrill scream moments before I connected with the surface. The impact knocked the air from my mouth and replaced it with heavy, cold water. A current grabbed my body, sucking me into an underwater hurricane. I tried to drive the cold water from my mouth as I reached for the surface, but I lost the remainder of air in my lungs. I panicked, kicking and clawing at the water as it attacked me. I reached for the surface again, but I couldn't distinguish up from down anymore. Fear made me frantic. The need to breathe was tearing at my lungs. Then, right before the water could claim me forever, right before my body gave in to the desperate need to inhale, a hand latched on to my arm and pulled me away from the black abyss.

In a flash I was met with fresh night air. Someone had a hold of me and guided my body toward the shore while I convulsively coughed up water.

"Don't panic, just breathe," a male voice said gently.

My head rested against wet brown fabric, and my hands clung to the dark sleeves of a loose shirt underneath it. Arms held tightly around me. They were strong arms—arms that had rescued me from the liquid death that had almost taken me. Between the lingering fear and the cold, it was hard to let go of those arms, even after I was carefully rolled on to cool earth.

Eventually, the coughing subsided, and my eyes focused on the rich dirt that lay beneath me: black

sand, filled with thousands of tiny crystal-like parti-
cles. I raked my fingers through it as I breathed.
You're safe now, I reminded myself. *You're safe.*

The hand of my savior softly circled my back as
I recovered. My throat burned and so did my nasal
cavity as the oxygen passed freely through them, but
it had never felt better to be surrounded with air. I
willed myself to move, eager to see the man who'd
saved my life.

For a moment, my heart stopped. It actually
stopped pumping altogether.

And then, it made up for the lost seconds by
beating entirely too fast, racing to push me into
awareness—to push me into action.

"You!" I pawed out from under the body that
leaned over me, drawing the sword from my side, still
half-lying on the ground. "Get away from me!"

The familiar porcelain mask I had once adored
concealed the face of the man I had learned to hate.
The beast was here; Edmund was here, standing over
me.

I was quick to meet his pale throat with the
steel of my blade.

"Don't be frightened," he said.

His voice was melodious, smooth like velvet. It
drew my eyes to his lips. It was then that I noticed
the mask was not quite the same. The porcelain
mask I remembered no longer covered his entire face.
The lines were the same, following the shape of his
face, but they ended slightly above his lips now. It
was the first time I had seen his lips fully, the first
time I'd seen the shape of his chin.

My knuckles whitened around the hilt of the sword while I deliberated my next move. Why did my rescuer have to be *him*?

I glared at Edmund, ignoring his perfectly arched lips and strong chin this time. I looked past the pale mask into the darkness of his eyes. On our last encounter, he had been more illusion than reality. He had morphed his eye color to mimic an electric green—a color I found most comforting, the color of Finn's eyes. But now, his eyes were his own—dark pupils floating in deep pools of chocolate. Those eyes unnerved me to my bone.

I remained frozen in defense below him, half propped up with one arm while the other held my blade. Even with the steel resting against the skin of his neck, he had the upper hand. He was stronger and stood above me; I was weak and trapped below. If I wanted to kill him, I had better do it fast. *Commit*, I thought. *See it through.*

But before I had a chance to draw a drop of blood, he knocked the blade from his neck and forced my exhausted body flat against the ground. In seconds, the hilt was twisted from my fingers and my arms were pinned behind my neck. I squirmed, trying to escape the force that held me down. He leaned closer to my body, pressing his forearm against my collarbone. I'd missed my chance. Now I was completely powerless to his strength.

"You wish to kill me?" he questioned sarcastically. "Never hesitate."

I tensed, readying myself for a blow that never came. He drifted back, allowing me to stand. Why was he letting me stand? Why was I still conscious?

Was he waiting for me to cower underneath him? To offer him my soul? What did he want?

"Now, try again," he said.

He was crazy. Mad. He had to be. Why else would he encourage me to attack? I needed to get away while I still had a chance.

I took off running.

There was a rustle behind me as I dodged through the forest, but I didn't look back. Even running, I felt like I was moving in slow motion. The mass of trees around me was endless. And no matter how much energy I put into my legs, they didn't seem to move fast enough. I was stuck in a nightmare, running as fast as humanly possible but getting nowhere. The sound of his boots flying over the forest floor grew closer and closer. And then the sound was right behind me.

He caught up to my speed without breaking a sweat. My escape attempt had been useless. Arms flew around my waist, pulling me back before forcing me against a tree. His power and strength were irrefutable, but that didn't stop me from putting up a fight.

I felt rage so intense it drove me to a moment of sheer madness. I hit him, using my fists like jackhammers, but his body was as solid as the tree behind me. My fists throbbed with pain, and my back stung from the rough bark scrapping against my skin. He trapped my arms to my sides, completely pinning me to the tree.

"Let me go! Get your hands off me!" I screamed, but I knew he wouldn't.

"Be still, Clarabella." That was all he said.

I kept squirming under his grip until my body finally tired, drooping like a ragdoll against the tree. With all my efforts, he never loosened his grip. Instead, he swiftly scooped me up and carried me back through the path I'd created, back to the waterfall.

What did he want with me? I guess that didn't really matter. No matter what it was, I still needed to escape. That's what I needed to focus on—getting away. But how could I take him down? If I became free again, I could rip the pendant from my neck and use the dagger as my weapon, but that might take seconds that I didn't have. Would it be faster to get to my sword? Was it still in the grass where it was forced out of my hand? It didn't seem to help much before, but then again, I'd hesitated. And I never hesitate. My eyes were fixated on the forest floor as I tried to come up with a plan. There was brush everywhere, a few large branches I could possibly use. But I would have to lift them fast and high to hit his head. And would a blow like that even bring him down? He was so strong.

As we neared the sound of moving water, I saw for the first time that we were not alone. There was a fire I hadn't noticed before and about eight dark-skinned men resting around it. Were they Edmund's soldiers? They appeared much older than soldiers, with deep wrinkles and heads filled with silver hair. A few of them glanced our way when we came into the light but quickly fell back into their previous state of rest.

"Put me down!" I screamed, over and over.

Edmund didn't blink or speak a word, but finally he set me gently on my feet once we reached the lake.

The hair on my arms stood up, like I was an angry cat about to pounce. It would have been nice, being a cat and all. I would have enjoyed scratching his eyes out or ripping apart his flesh, but my scowl would have to do for now. I scanned the campground, desperately seeking my sword, but came up empty. All I had now was my cross pendant, so it would have to do. I tore it from my neck and squeezed it to life. The bright blue beam sliced through the dark air, extending into the sharp dagger.

"What do you want with me?" I hissed.

"I desire to help you, Clara."

"Help me? Ha!" I shifted my feet slowly away from him.

He chuckled to himself as I spoke, seemingly amused by my reaction.

"Don't taunt me like it's sport. And don't you think you stand a chance at gaining my soul. You can kill my body, but neither my soul nor any part of me will ever be yours. I can promise you that." I spit the words out so matter-of-factly that I surprised even myself.

He gracefully moved closer to me, filling in the gap I was trying hard to create. "Clarabella." He said my name slowly and smoothly, sending a chill to my skin. "I'm not going to kill you, and my wish is not to take your soul."

"Lies!" I screamed. "Stop feeding me your lies! I know who you really are. You are one of them! You kill the innocent and you prey on the weak. I despise you!"

He stepped even closer, moving so swiftly that I flinched. He stood now with his chest only inches from the point of my dagger. *Stab him,* I told myself. *Stab him, now.* But I couldn't. Something in me wouldn't allow it. I could see that his pupils were dilated and he was glaring now. He wasn't afraid of me in the least, but I was of him. My bravery was slipping.

"Listen to me," he said through gritted teeth. "Do not speak of what you do not know. These are not lies. It is in your best interest to believe what I have to tell you."

My eyes searched for refuge from the intensity of his stare, finding it among the dancing flames of the fire behind him. It wasn't until then that I noticed her. Just past the fire's blaze, beyond the flicker of light, was a girl, not much older than myself, painted from head to foot in gold. Her eyes were fixed on mine, glowing with a strange beauty as she neared. Momentarily my feelings of fear and anxiety were masked with pure curiosity. Who was this girl standing so quietly in the night?

Her hair was full and frizzy, fashioned up so that it lay on the top of her head, sweeping over her narrow forehead. She had very small, delicate features and bright yellow-gold eyes. Her chest was bound with a bandana-shaped piece of leathery material, and a small leather skirt hung from her hips, ending slightly above her knees. She almost looked like a statue, but she was much too beautiful to be made of metal.

She stepped completely from the shadows of the trees and quietly walked over to me, keeping her golden eyes on me the entire time. I was still mesmerized—calmed by her presence. And that confused me. Edmund took a few steps back to allow room for her to come between us. When she stood only inches away, she placed her hands on my cheeks. I lowered the blade of my dagger, letting down my defense completely.

A natural response would have been to turn away, to fear her, but there was something kind in her eyes, something innocent about her entire demeanor that kept me from moving. Instead, I watched her scan every feature of my face. There was a twinkle of happiness in her eyes, and then a smile formed from the curve of her golden lips.

"*Hai os ollos do seu pai,*" she said.

"Excuse me?" I asked, bewildered.

"*Hai os ollos do seu pai.*"

Edmund cleared his throat, catching my awareness for a moment. "She said you have your father's eyes."

My gaze quickly darted back to the golden girl before me. "You knew my father?"

"*Eu o conecia ben. El loitou para salvar o meu pobo. El me contrabandeados para a seguridade,*" she replied.

Edmund's body shifted beside me, and then he began to translate. "She knew him well. He fought to save her people. He made sure that she was smuggled to safety," he said. "She is forever in his debt."

There was a long pause as I stood staring blankly at the two of them. Thinking. Questioning.

35

She knew my father? If that were true, she could very well be the last person my father spoke with. The thought was both exciting and terrifying, all at the same time.

"Me, Kalani." Her golden hands tapped her chest softly, and then moved to grab my hand. "You, guardian. Chosen one."

Kalani. I had heard this name before. She was the princess of Zy.

When I was young my father spoke of our allies, the Zyons, and said that one day our kingdoms would unite the south with all of the northern regions. A marriage between Zy and Everest—the princess of Zy and the prince of Everest. This marriage had been decided upon by the Senate, a group of elders chosen by the people to ensure our kingdom thrived under any rule, under any king. The senators had proclaimed that the union would join this world together, and the king had agreed. At the time, I was so young it meant nothing to me, only politics. If I had known then how it would affect me now—how it would affect Finn…well, I would have thought differently. Kalani still held my hand, waiting patiently for me to process.

"Do you know where my father is?" I asked finally.

"*Tebras vir. Matar o meu pobo,*" she said. "Dark ones come. Kill my people. Enslave my people. *Exercito de garda foron emboscados…*" I saw her look to Edmund for help with the translation.

"Your father and the army of guardians were ambushed shortly after they arrived in Zy," he said. Kalani made a gesture with her hands, signaling Edmund to finish her story. He nodded, and then continued. "Your father fought bravely to see that Kalani and a group of elders escaped to sea."

"Father brave one," she added, placing both palms to my shoulders. "Father save me."

This changes everything. Maytide had said that she was an elder. These were her people. The Zyons. Had Maytide been a part of the group my father saved?

I had never spent much time around a Zyon. Their people stayed north of Everest, traveling only to the northern islands on occasion. They were people of simplicity, my father used to say. Their land provided everything they needed to survive. Their princess, Kalani, was said to be the gem of the forest. Now I could easily see why she was so highly regarded. Everything about her was lovely—enchanting even. The way she moved, spoke, it was effortless and graceful. My eyes were on her, eager for more answers, for more information.

"Why are you here? Why are you with him?" My eyes switched to Edmund as I asked the questions.

"Masked man keep us safe," she said. "Help our people."

"Him?"

"Masked man help," she repeated.

My sight remained fixed on Edmund, still surprised by what I was hearing. "Do you plan to gain their trust and devour them as you did with me?"

"Of course not. And that was never the case with you, Clara."

"Right," I said sarcastically.

"Whatever you think you know is incorrect."

"Listen to masked man. He help you," Kalani added.

Kalani stepped back and pushed Edmund forward so that he stood directly in front of me again. Then she casually strolled back to the fire.

Again, I was alone with a mad man, but I wasn't frightened. My fear had been pushed aside by the anger that filled me now. Each breath he took increased that anger. I hated that I hadn't killed him when I had the chance. So for him to have my attention, any attention other than the attention needed to kill him, felt wrong on every account.

"Tell me, Edmund, if you are so great at helping everyone, why didn't you help my father? You knew where he was. Why not free him and the Zyons?"

"I was unaware that anyone had survived," he said. "I found Kalani and the elders by chance, a few nights after the masquerade. I was looking for you, but instead I discovered them hiding in the forest of pine light."

"And I'm supposed to believe this?"

He stepped closer.

"I know you have no reason to trust me, but I beg you to try," he said. "It is true that I have not always been good, but I am no longer that man."

I grimaced at his nearness. Even though he saved me from drowning, even though he said he wanted to protect me, I had no reason to trust him. He had betrayed me on every level. But there was something else that tore at my stomach when I looked at him; there was a conflict within him. Was this a bad man capable of good, or was this a good man capable of bad? I had witnessed him as both.

All of my memories had returned to me the day I destroyed Victor, including the memories of Edmund before the attack. He had been good once...

Knowing what I did now, I couldn't believe he had ever stirred any kind of feelings of desire in me. But in the castle, he had. Just as all guardians, he had been given a gift, but his was quite a powerful one. His gift gave him power over perception. With this ability he could alter another's consciousness, including thoughts, feelings, and emotions. He could have adjusted how I perceived and understood everything. The only question was, had he? Had everything been an illusion? Or was something real? I honestly didn't know, but from the moment I caught him conspiring with Victor, I convinced myself that it had all been artificial.

He himself had been a victim of power, seduced by the purest form of evil, convinced that he could have it all if he joined the dark side. So all of my feelings had to have been linked to his power. He had to have persuaded me to think and feel those feelings for him.

Even though I could barely remember his face, I remembered that he had been handsome, lean, and strong. I thought this from the moment we had met as children. He was the son of a great guardian, William Drake—a guardian who had fought side by side with my father. Edmund's destiny was meant to be great too. So they had said. But things went awfully wrong for him. When he was just a boy, his mother and father were struck with fever, which killed them both in a single winter. Edmund was sent to live with his uncle, a brutal man who had no love in his heart. He abused Edmund as if it were sport. Edmund was overworked and malnourished, beaten and cursed. No one could possibly know the pain and suffering he lived through those years.

The guardians eventually found out about his uncle, of course, and removed Edmund from the hell his uncle had created for him. The uncle was even put on trial in front of the king and Senate of Everest. We weren't sure what his sentence was, but I know that no one ever saw him again. We assumed he was thrown in prison or banished from our island.

My parents were the first to offer Edmund a home. I was only twelve when this happened. They brought him to our home like a stray puppy, cleaning him up, feeding him, and giving him all the love two people could possibly give. They tried every day to undo the hurt that had been inflicted on him.

But I could see the pain in his eyes, from the very start. It was a deep pain, far greater than any physical pain could be. Occasionally he would lose his temper, but it wasn't something he could control. It wasn't his fault, really. He wasn't born with this rage; it had been beaten into him. For the longest time, he didn't speak. He just stared, taking in the world around him. Mom believed his uncle had punished him for speaking. My father thought he might never talk because of it. But then one day he spoke. It was a day I remembered well.

It had been an ordinary day. I had gone out gathering cloudberries and blueberries for my mother with Edmund. He always seemed to follow me around, watching me, studying me. Just before I had a full basket of berries, I bent down to pick a few more, but my reach was met with a sharp pain. My mind didn't comprehend what had happened until I heard the light rattle of the snake's tail. Edmund jumped into action, killing the snake in seconds and rushing to my side. I remembered the pain so clearly, my hand burning as if encompassed with fire. Without hesitation, Edmund pressed his lips against the wound, pulling the pain away. I was weak and light-headed when he helped me back home, but I remembered him whispering, "Don't leave me, Clarabella. Please, don't leave me." That was the first time I heard his voice.

As I thought back to that time, my heart softened a bit, allowing leniency for his recent fury. I hadn't thought about our childhood in a long time. Was that same sweet boy still in there somewhere? Was it possible that Edmund wasn't *all* bad?

The trees were mere ghosts in the woods now that the wind had died down. Beams of moonlight glistened from the lake while the fire to our right continued to cast its warm glow on the shadowed men snoozing by it. There was enough light from the pine needles to see the depth of the forest. It seemed endless, much like the questions in my mind.

I took a few steps back, crunching the brittle grass at my feet. I focused on the sound of the waterfall to clear my head. My nerves were rattled, but I had to face him. I had so many questions, so many things I wanted to know. I turned to address Edmund, once more.

"What do you want with me?"

An emotion stirred in his eyes, one that I couldn't figure out.

"You were brought back to this world for a reason, Clara. The sword from the tiger lily only presents itself for those worthy of its cause," he said.

"What cause?"

He shifted, seemingly glancing at the lake for a moment. "Come, there is something you must see."

Edmund's posture remained tall while he crossed the campsite to the water's edge. He didn't check to see if I followed; I guess he knew that I would. I tried not to walk too closely, in case he decided to turn abruptly. I felt that it was best to keep a constant distance from him, no matter the good intentions he claimed to have.

Kalani appeared pleased that I had willingly followed Edmund, dropping her satchel to the ground to throw her thin arms around me. She backed away, tugging me closer to Edmund and to the edge of the bank where her satchel now lay.

"Gift. I show you," she said, reaching into the open bag.

Kalani pulled out a small green apple and held it between both of her graceful hands. She slowly brought the fruit close to her lips, but not quite touching, and then softly blew. As her breath touched the skin of the apple, it turned to shiny gold. If this hadn't been the lost world, if I hadn't seen the magic in this place firsthand, then I might have jumped with surprise. But this wasn't my first encounter with the unexplainable. Here in the lost world, anything could happen. And it usually did.

"Gift. I show you," she repeated, holding the apple in front of me. "Bite."

This didn't seem like a good idea, at first. I mean, how well did I know her, really? But as I looked at her, really looked at her, I thought of my father and how he had risked so much to save her and her people. So how could I not trust her?

"Okay," I finally agreed, accepting the strange gift.

I slid my fingers over the skin of the apple, noticing that the change in color hadn't affected its texture. I could smell the freshness of the fruit as I brought it close to my lips. It smelled like an apple, so I opened my mouth and took a bite.

At first it was like biting into any other apple, except it was exceptionally sweet. Sweet like a caramel or candied apple. But as I chewed, I was mentally preparing myself for something, because with magic, something big always came after the nothing. After I had successfully swallowed the first bite, Kalani gently pushed me to the water's edge and directed my focus down into the dark water of the lake.

"*Mostrar os seus ollos o que ela debe ver*," she said.

Her hand extended to mine, reaching for the golden apple. As soon as it was in her hand, she dropped it in the water. It seemed pointless. I was expecting it to change forms or burst into flames, fly or something crazy, but now the apple was resting at the bottom of the lake. Was that what she meant to happen? Did I miss something?

Suddenly, the water beamed with blue light. It looked as though the apple had exploded into hundreds of tiny stars below the water's surface. Each tiny star multiplied by the second, creating a more brilliant light than before. It was a spectacular sight, one that reminded me of a time long ago when I was shown something very similar to its brilliancy.

I remembered it clearly. I was barely five and my parents took me to a lake, much like this one, hidden within the forests of Everest. They took me there to witness the natural light display produced by the disturbed plankton in the water. It was the first time they explained to me the importance of good and evil, of light and the darkness. My mother had said that we were just like the plankton, swimming blindly in dark water—that it was when we shined that we could do our most good, that we could bring light to the darkness. They wanted me to understand the importance of even the smallest of organisms and know that light could be found in any place, just like it could be found in anyone, if you looked hard enough.

The apple's burst of light began to come together under the water, merging to form fuzzy images like the kind you would see on an old black-and-white television set.

Edmund stood tall behind us, casting his lean shadow over the water. "Ask your question. Look past the ripples for your answer," he said.

I knew exactly what I wanted to ask. My knees bent, slowly dropping to the soft sand that lined the lake. I sat there, hunched over the rippling water, until the question rolled from my lips.

"Is my father alive?"

Images of screaming men, women, and children came into focus in the blue light of the water. All wore metal collars around their necks, chained together like animals. Leather whips split through the air, cutting through the skin of the elders. I saw my father's face appear. His cheeks were hollow, and dark circles shadowed his eyes, but it was him. I would recognize his eyes anywhere, even in the darkest of places.

The light faded back to the dark water of before.

"Father!" I gasped. My knees sank further into the wet embankment while quiet sobs rasped in my throat. I somehow managed to whimper words through the tightness. "Take me there—take me to him, please!"

I felt Edmund's hand trail along the ridge of my spine, patting my back lightly as to soothe my pain. He kneeled down beside me, carefully guiding my head to his shoulder. I instinctively pulled away, finding my way back to my feet.

"Don't," was all I could say. I didn't think I could handle him being that nice to me. I didn't trust him.

He rose from the damp earth, keeping a noticeable distance. "As you wish."

I found myself shifting back and forth on my feet, and then pacing between him and Kalani. *I have to do something. I have to get to him.* My thoughts suddenly exploded from my mouth in the form of a plea.

"Please...I have to go to my father. If you want to help me, you will take me there."

"There are things you must know. Things that have transpired since your absence."

"What?" My eyes filled with warm tears. What could I possibly need to know that was more important than finding my father?

"A new army has emerged," he said, his expression darkening. "Clara, I no longer govern this kingdom or anyone who resides in Everest. I abandoned the throne so that the rightful king might return to power. I wanted to make it right again. In doing so, I fear I have only angered the leader of the new army."

My head shook almost instantly. *Victor is dead,* I thought. *I know he is.* Victor's fall should have brought about the fall of the darkness. The entire kingdom should have found peace within itself.

"Victor is dead. Who stands to lead an army against Everest?"

"Yes, Victor perished, but his son lives."

"His son?"

"His son has raised an army to fight against the remainder of the guardians and to fulfill his father's dream of darkness. He has placed a price on your head. He knows of the prophecy…he knew that you would be brought back into this world. I have waited, searching for you, hoping to find you before his dark soldiers."

"You must be mistaken. How can Victor have a son when it's a well-known fact that the fallen can't reproduce?"

"That is what the guardians believe. That is what I believed, until I saw his son with my own eyes."

46

"But, how can that be possible?"

"I realize you must have a lot of questions, for there is a lot to be told," he said. "But first you must understand that these answers lie far in the past."

"Please, tell me what you know."

Edmund nodded.

"Long before you and I were ever born—over five hundred years ago, the last female guardian roamed the earth. She had the same power that you possess, the power to kill the fallen. But before she could kill Victor, she was seduced by his charm and beauty. The young guardian managed to escape Victor's grasp, but by then, it was already too late. She was with child. Her guilt consumed her. She had not only failed at ridding this world of Victor, but she had given birth to the child who would potentially destroy this world and the next." He lowered his voice. "The night she gave birth to this child, she took her own life. Her body was found the next day, hanging from a tree just outside the castle wall. Behind the tree lay a basket with a crying baby wrapped inside."

He paused, clearing his throat, and then continued. "A family of guardians took the baby in, raising him as their own. They named the child Erik. But no one knew of the child's true identity. No one knew he was the son of the fallen."

"Erik," I mused. "But this happened over five hundred years ago. Did no one notice that Erik never aged?"

"Even though he is immortal like the fallen, he aged like a guardian until his twenty-fifth birthday— the prime age for a mortal. If Erik never aged, he would have been useless to Victor, frozen as a baby until the end of time. But that was not the case."

"How could he live all that time without anyone discovering who he really was?"

"There's no way to really know, it was so long ago, but we believe he went into hiding or joined Victor in Hades until everyone he knew had passed. He only emerged a few years before the attack of Everest. He gained everyone's trust, which wasn't hard to do since he was half guardian. He had the gift to prove it. In those two years he managed to join the king's army, under your father's command no less. And no one knew, because there has never been a half-breed…a dark child before."

"What is his gift? What are we up against?"

"Persuasion. He has the ability to persuade the weak of mind with a single touch or stare."

"Persuasion," I muttered to myself.

It made sense. I thought back to all the times I had been around Erik. I had never really been attracted to him, but whenever I'd been around him, I felt strangely otherwise. When he would touch me, I would hear his voice in my head almost like my own subconscious insisting that I wanted to be near him. Every time this happened, my mind would blur and then fill with strange thoughts or ideas—thoughts that I would never have when I wasn't in his presence. Now I knew it was simply Erik using his abilities to persuade me to want him, to be near him.

Before I had learned of my background and the reality of magic, I had no idea that Erik was causing me to think these thoughts. Living in a world where things like that don't happen—it was easy to ignore it. That's why most people are blind to the abilities and gifts that our kind possess. The good and the bad. Sometimes humans can feel it, but they don't believe it because it's not tangible. The day I felt it, the day I noticed something wasn't right and pushed it away, was the day Erik came at me. He knew that he couldn't control me or persuade me anymore, because I finally fought against it. Even though I had no idea what I fought against.

"So there aren't any others like him?"

"No, the women marked as fallen cannot produce children. That is part of their curse…infertility. They can only join in turning others to create more of their kind, but if a man who is marked seduces a guardian, then a baby can be conceived," he said. "The Zyons call them children of the dark. Since there is only a female guardian born every five hundred years, we have some ability to prevent this from happening. That is why it's so important to protect you."

"You don't want the same thing that happened to Erik's mom to happen to me."

"Correct."

"How do you know all of this?"

"The night of the masquerade, Victor told me everything. He told me of his plans for this world, how he had spent centuries scheming and planning for what was soon to come. I only wish I could have told you this, that night. I wish you knew the truth before you ran."

I looked past him, taking in everything he had just said, trying to piece it all together. The man I despised held more answers than I could have possibly known, and even with all the hate that festered inside of me, I wanted to talk more to him. I wanted to find out everything.

"I still don't understand. Why did Victor ever want me? Why does Erik want me now? It makes no sense. If they knew all along that I could destroy them, why risk coming near me?"

"The fallen only have a chance to reproduce with a female guardian every five hundred years. Victor not only wanted your soul, he wanted you to give him another offspring. Don't you see? You are the key: either to ending this war, or to bringing about a new era of darkness. Erik wishes to finish what his father started. He wants the souls of all the great guardians, their powers—but more importantly, he wants you. He plans to capture you so that you may spawn a dark child," he said. "Evil will flourish if he is not stopped. This world and your world will no longer be as we know them to be. The prophecy is our only hope."

His reaction was not one that I expected. He seemed strangely upset, like this really mattered to him. I thought he was on their side.

The prophecy. Maybe I could get more out of him than I did Maytide.

"What do you know of the prophecy?" I questioned.

"It is said that a great darkness will sweep the land if the chosen does not defeat the one who leads the fallen. That no light will touch the soil of this kingdom for five hundred years. And darkness will spread through this world to the next, bringing pain to those who do not surrender. Only the chosen guardian can bring an end to this prophecy."

"What else do you know? Does it say that someone will die?"

"That I cannot tell you. What I know of the prophecy is all legend, passed down from generation to generation."

"I need to know more."

"And you will. Tomorrow we journey to a place that holds the prophecy. Tomorrow we will both find the truth behind the legend."

I paced the edge of the lake, taking in all the information given to me. It was a lot to process. My father was alive. Erik was creating an army. I was part of an ancient prophecy. And supposedly Edmund wasn't evil to his core. I still hadn't made my mind up about that one.

Edmund retreated from the lake while I wrestled with these thoughts.

There was a slight rustle from behind as he worked quickly at the edge of the forest, draping a large brown cloth over a low-hanging pine branch. My gaze darted to him a few times while he secured the four edges of the cloth to the ground with wooden stakes. He made it seem so effortless. But what did I expect? His arms were pure muscle, more like steel than flesh.

"Are you hungry?" he asked, stepping from the newly structured tent.

"I'm fine," was my automatic response. Even though I could feel a bit of emptiness in my stomach, my head full of questions distracted my ability to register any notion of hunger. "I just need to be alone. I have a lot to think about."

"If that is your wish," he said quietly.

I nodded and he bowed in response.

For a moment that small gesture took me back to our time together in the ballroom of Everest, to the night he twirled me around the dance floor as if I were his. I shook the image away, said goodnight, and stepped into the small space of the tent. Tonight this thin fabric was all that separated me from the masked man who had spawned so many nightmares over the last year. I'd thought I hated him. Now, I didn't know what to think. Was he good? Was he bad? Should I trust him?

I decided to give him the smallest amount of trust I could give without falling into dangerous territory. It was my only option in order to find out more about the prophecy and to find my father. Just a small amount of trust…

The light snoring of the elders blended with the crackle of the fire, and finally, my own conscious relaxed into sleep.

4

DEAL

I WOKE SUDDENLY IN THE NIGHT. THE SOUND OF TWIGS breaking outside the tent caught my immediate attention. The sound was loud enough to overpower the rush of the water, so I knew that whatever it was had walked directly past my tent into the trees behind it. I rolled to a sitting position and peeked through the slit of doorway.

The fire had died down to a glow, and the Zyons lay sound asleep on the ground around it. I looked to the woods where I had heard the noise and saw light moving through the trees. Without hesitation, I crawled out of the tent, stood silently, and headed into the woods, following the light carefully and quietly.

The wavering light moved through the night air, following the curves of the lake for almost a mile, and then came to a dead stop. I moved from tree to tree until two figures came into view.

"I left him right around here," said a tall, lanky boy. "I'm sure of it."

Edmund stood next to the boy, making him look even lankier.

"You're sure of this?"

The kid muttered something to himself, nervously pacing back and forth with the torch. He looked like he was about to unravel. Then a wiry old man hobbled from the depths of the forest, ending his nervous frenzy. As the man neared, the torch was raised high enough to show every spot of dirt on the man's face, including the grime in his matted hair.

"Why have you come?" Edmund asked. "You were to stay watch at Zyon. That is what we discussed."

"Yes, yes...I know. But I came to warn you," said the man. "I came to warn you of the dark prince."

"I have made my deal with the prince, and he knows I will honor it."

"But, sire—"

"I asked you not to call me that," Edmund interrupted.

The old man shook his head, grumbling under his breath for a second, before he continued. "Surrendering to him will not save the female guardian. And we cannot wage a battle against him. Not with our shrinking numbers. Unless your plan is to die a senseless death, you should back down."

"It would not be senseless." Edmund's tone sounded as if he were suppressing anger.

"You know the legend. He needs her to spawn the dark child. If the chosen one's blood is not shed, this kingdom will surely go into darkness. Dying for her will not save this kingdom. And it will not save her."

"It is legend, not fact. Watch the dark prince. Watch his every move, and find a weakness in his fortress. Find a way in so that we may set the Zyons free. Let me worry about the rest," he said. "I will come to you when the time is right. No more lectures on legends or myths. I will fight for her."

"Then you have sentenced yourself to death."

"So be it."

Edmund broke away; his stride was long and quick as he headed back toward camp. The old man stood and shook his head disapprovingly as he motioned for the kid with the torch to follow him. I hid behind a log as everyone parted. After Edmund was a good distance away, I resumed following him back on the trail from before.

What was I supposed to think of this? Edmund knew much more than he'd revealed. Why was he so eager to fight for me? Was it true that he wanted to help? Terror struck me as I realized the man spoke of my future. And it didn't sound like a good one.

The hike back to camp felt like it took much longer than the curious journey away, but soon I could see the glow of the campfire through the trees. Surprisingly, as soon as the camp came into view, Edmund veered off the path, making his way to the lake.

I watched from behind an old pine, studying him as he removed layers of clothing. He waded into the shadows of the water, tossing the last of his clothing behind him. His back and chest were marked with deep lines, scars it seemed, but as the water trickled down, mingling shining rivulets with whitened scars, they appeared as marks of beauty rather than pain.

His head turned left, and then right, carefully surveying the camp behind him as his hands moved to his mask, lingering along the edge of the porcelain in uncertainty, before removing it from his face. I squinted, trying to see what had been hidden all this time from me, but could only make out a faint silhouette. There he was, his face completely exposed to every living creature in the forest, yet I was the only one taking notice, the only one trying to see it. I found myself wanting a better view.

He tossed the mask to the bank, and then dunked under water.

A few seconds went by before he resurfaced. Edmund appeared vulnerable without his mask, less of the monster I thought him to be. It was like watching a lion in secret, waiting to see what the beast of the forest would do when he thought no one was looking. But at this moment, Edmund didn't seem like a beast at all. Now he'd transformed into a graceful creature of the night, gliding through the water like it was a part of him. He blended perfectly with the beauty of the lake in the forest. Why couldn't I break my stare?

I watched him dunk in and out of the water, combing dark strands of glossy hair back from his face. His whole body glistened. Was it the moon beaming against the water on his skin or the glow of the plankton stirring around him? I couldn't decide—I just kept staring, waiting for his face to come into focus. I couldn't pull my eyes away.

He started to swim his way back to the bank.

I quickly repositioned my body so that I sat with my back against the trunk of the pine tree and my knees curled into my chest in an effort to stay hidden. There a final soft splashing sound, followed by footsteps in the sand. I waited for the sound of his steps to fade into the songs of the crickets before I glanced around the tree.

His mask and clothes were no longer on the bank; he was nowhere in sight.

"How long have you been here?"

I flinched, turning around quickly.

"Edmund. I…just…" I cleared my throat, embarrassed and frightened all at once.

He looked down through his mask with spiteful eyes.

"Not long. I…" I was disappointed that I still sounded nervous. I stood, as an attempt to appear less intimidated, but from the unwavering scowl of his lips, I knew that I had failed.

"Did you follow me?"

"No," I lied, again. And it was still unconvincing.

"What did you see? Answer me!" he growled. It was a harsh tone, sending a quick tremor over me.

I stood there, staring blankly into the darkness between us now. I couldn't tell him that I overheard him talking about my future, and I couldn't tell him that I saw his face, even if it was from a distance. He interrupted my frantic thoughts, which were still searching for a good lie.

"Get out of my sight," he hissed. "Go, now!"

I still had no words.

I turned and quickly stormed off, following the small path back to camp. I wanted to run again, but I knew that I needed him to find my father, and for that, I hated him.

The tent seemed smaller now, more like a prison, but I reminded myself that this was the only way. I tried to sleep, but the tighter I closed my eyes, the more awake I became. I tossed and turned, unable to get comfortable in the grass under me. I watched as shadows flickered across the cloth of the tent, cast by tall plants swaying in the night breeze. I noticed a figure pacing the ground only a few yards away from my tent. It looked like Edmund, but I wasn't about to peep, not ever again. I stared at his moving shadow for almost an hour before my head slumped down to the earth and I drifted into a dreamless state of sleep. Finally, my mind could rest.

-5-

TEMPER

Morning brought a new scene. I was greeted by the pearly white smile of Kalani as soon as I stepped from my tent. She pulled me over to the fire where the elders were gathered, eating an array of berries and fish. They all nodded their heads and smiled, speaking a few words that I didn't understand. Their gestures were friendly, so I figured they were saying nice things. One man, who had a long, scraggily beard and three red lines painted on his forehead, motioned for me to sit down, so I grinned politely and sat next to him. The man who sat slumped beside him offered a strange container to me, but I declined after smelling the strong scent of spirits on him. I had tried drinking rum once or twice before, but the flavor never set well with me. He handed me a small woven basket next, containing a rather large slice of cooked fish. The fish was still warm and smelled of strong herbs. I didn't pass on this.

"Thank you," I said, placing a bite of the fish in my mouth.

Everyone looked at me and nodded to acknowledge my words, but no one spoke. I glanced over the men, getting a good look at them for the first time since my arrival in the lost world. Much like the bearded man, all eight elders had three red lines painted on their foreheads. I wondered what that meant. *Is it simply a distinct symbol of the elders?* Yet another question I didn't know how to ask.

While I finished the last of the fish, I began to scan the camp for signs of Edmund, but I didn't see a trace of him anywhere. *Good*, I thought. *Delay the inevitable awkwardness as long as possible.*

I had just turned my attention back to my food when goose bumps erupted on my arms, and a feeling of uncomfortable agitation settled over me. Through almost a sixth sense, I knew at once that Edmund was watching me. I still couldn't see him anywhere, but I felt his eyes studying me. The hair standing on end, the skin crawling—it was the same feeling I got every time he looked at me. He was using his power of perception to alter what my eyes could and couldn't see. He was lurking somewhere close, watching me like a ghost. My cheeks reddened. Was he standing behind me? Was that wind that just ruffled my hair actually him, breathing down my neck? I wasn't going to let him have that kind of power over me. I threw down the food in my hands and marched around the camp, trying to pinpoint his location, but I felt his presence all around me.

"Show yourself!" I demanded.

Everyone around the fire silenced immediately, waiting for the train wreck. Their eyes darted over to the tree by my tent. *Aha!* So everyone could see him except me. I was the only one whose mind was being tampered with.

"You have no right to get inside my mind!" I shouted at the tree, feeling equal parts angry and humiliated.

There was still no answer from him, and he didn't appear. Goose bumps formed again on my arms; an exhilarating tingle swept over my shoulder.

"Edmund! I know you're there. Stop toying with my perception! Do you hear me?"

Still silence.

I stomped my way directly under the tree that the Zyons were still watching warily. "Why should I be surprised?" I called up. "You hide everything. First your stupid mask, then your secret meeting—now this! You're such a coward!"

My next insult seized in my throat as a hand gripped my neck and Edmund appeared out of thin air beside me.

"I am no coward," he hissed through clenched teeth, his brown eyes boring into mine.

Gasping through a crushed windpipe, I wanted to fight him off, but I was momentarily paralyzed by his eyes and the memory they unearthed—of Edmund, throwing my weak body among red waves of sheets and locking me in the castle of Everest.

His fingers around my neck sent a pulse down my spine. Fear and loathing always masked a small amount of an unexplainable attraction: the allure of who he was and the mystery of who he had become.

The entire incident lasted only a moment. Edmund's rage-filled eyes softened as suddenly as he'd appeared, transforming to warm pools of brown— the big brown eyes I'd known as a child. His hand loosened quickly, as if he suddenly realized the wrong he had done, and then he backed away.

"Forgive me." His shoulders dropped, and he turned his masked face from me.

Is he serious? This was the second time his hand had been wrapped around my neck, blocking the air from my lungs, and he expected me to forgive him?

"What is your problem?" I wanted to shout, but my voice was raspy from the struggle.

He stepped forward to respond, quickly, drawing so very close. I heard a breath of air escape his lips. My breathing became rapid as he neared. Was he going to assault me again?

"It will not happen again."

And then as swiftly as he appeared, he walked away.

I had no words to describe the feelings I had after he was no longer near me. And not a single clear thought formed in my mind. My subconscious rattled about, darting around my growing fear and anger as it looked for reflection. Why had he been spying on me? What did he have to gain from getting inside my head? Edmund was impossible to read! How was I to know what to believe with him? Should I trust what I'd overheard him say the night before? Or continue to hate him for the pain he'd caused me in the past?

I rubbed my neck with the sweaty palm of my hand, circling the tender place he'd clenched in fury. Out of the corner of my eye, I saw him stop where the trees turned to forest. He dropped one knee to the ground and lifted my sword in the same hands that had just threatened my existence.

Everything about him drove me crazy—mad, even. His conflicting actions, his contradicting words and tones. And as much as I despised the notion, I had to trust this mad man to some degree, or I was on my own. He was my only link to my father. He knew things that I needed to know, and I would have to stick around long enough to find out what those things were. No matter what he said or did, I was stuck.

I began to move, walking to put distance between myself and everyone else at camp. When I found myself back at the edge of the lake, my mind finally found its clarity. *He's still a beast,* I thought. *A real beast.*

And that was the only clarity I needed.

He had to force me into one of the narrow canoes when it was time to leave the camp.

I only put up a fight because he wanted me in the one that he led. I still wasn't sure if joining Edmund and his out-of-control temper was the right decision. I still wasn't sure if I'd compromised too much, just for the small hope of finding my father. So for him to force me in any direction didn't help matters. I tried to convince myself this was the right decision—that staying with the beast would pay off in the end. I had to try to believe that some miracle could happen.

The canoe was still rocking in the water when he pushed off from the bank. At least my struggle had made getting into the canoe a little challenging for him.

We followed the lake as it bent, twisting and turning in every direction. It was quiet except for the birds singing overhead and the occasional fish jumping from the water. That certainly got the Zyons to grumbling. There was no way to know what they said; I imagined they were complaining about hunger pains, but it could have been anything really. Through it all, Edmund never said a word, nor did I.

The canoes carried us quickly and efficiently north, past changing landscapes. Whenever we caught a land breeze, it carried the scent of honey mingled with earthy forest, but only briefly before the metallic lake smell overpowered it. The current did a lot of the work, pushing the canoes forward, but it took quite a bit of energy to steer them away from rocks and fallen trees that were embedded in the lake bottom. The elders grew tired in the heat of the day, but Edmund instructed us to keep moving.

The sun was high above us when we finally stopped. We had reached a part of the lake where the water was still and the bends were few. Kalani shouted to Edmund from the leading canoe, something in her native tongue, prompting him to speak for the first time since camp.

"Stay clear of the rocks," he said. "And make way to shore."

My shoes were drenched as I stepped to the bank, something I knew I would regret if we had to journey much further to our destination. And unfortunately, we did.

The location Edmund picked for camp was an odd choice. It was very narrow and very open— visible from the north, south, and west. But again, no one dared to fight his decision.

The trees here were not pine trees of light, but a tangle of different types of trees with thick green vegetation on the ground between them. With swampy land near the edge of the water and carpet-like grass all around, the landscape instantly reminded me of Louisiana. Ferns sprouted as big as full-grown men, and the overly saturated ground was home to cypress and redwood trees. Frogs croaked at each other, mosquitoes swarmed, water soaked my shoes—just like old Coushatta. Two raccoons fought over a crawfish hole, before scurrying into the wilderness behind us.

After the Zyons pulled the canoes from the lake, they carried them one by one over to a rotten tree that lay on its side, yards from the water. They carefully set the canoes down, hull side up, and positioned them so that they were no longer visible from the water's edge. Were we being followed? Until now, it hadn't crossed my mind that someone might be tracking us.

I stood awkwardly between the Zyons and the lake as we waited for Edmund's next instruction.

"Clara and I will be hiking to the mountain alone," he announced. "Kalani, you will stay here. Keep close to the elders at all times. We will return by dawn."

"We wait," she responded. She tossed a leather satchel to me. My hands instinctively flew out to catch it.

"Take," she said.

Inside the satchel was a small hand-woven blanket, golden in color, and a thicker woolen blanket, like the one used to construct my tent from the night before.

"You should keep this," I said, holding it back out to her. "You might need it."

She stepped closer to me, pushing the satchel against my chest. "You keep."

"Are you sure?"

"Keep, for you. Be safe and warm."

"Thanks." I looped the satchel over my shoulder. "You...you stay safe, too."

Edmund moved between us, shoving a leather sheath and the sword of Tiger Lily into my arms, before pulling Kalani a several yards away from me. His face was turned away as he began to speak in a whisper. I was glad to have a weapon once more—glad to know I could defend myself if Edmund's fury attacked again, but now I wanted to know what he was telling Kalani. What was he whispering? I tried to eavesdrop, but his words were lost in the abundant sounds of nature coming from the forest in front of us. Kalani's eyes wandered from his to mine and back again as he spoke, but she gave no clue as to the message being told.

Once again, I was aware that he was keeping something from me, but this time I wouldn't let it control my emotions. I didn't want another altercation, not when I was still nervous from the last. So I stood very still, silently waiting for his next move. When he finally turned to me, I made sure to keep my curious eyes from his. I wondered if he was aware of this. And I wondered if he could sense my resentment and fear.

"Let's go," he said, stepping back to me. I slid the cold steel into the sheath given to me, fastened it securely to my belt, and then obediently followed his command. There was no questioning him now.

As we walked away from the group, Edmund shouted back one last instruction to Kalani.

"Remember, stay close to the lake, and be sure to start a fire in the eve of the night."

It was an unusual thing to suggest, with the camp being in such an open area, but I kept my mouth shut and conceded to following him alone into the trees.

Everything was covered in moss. The ground was soft and overgrown with spongy green and yellow plants, reminding me even more of the bayou that was one time my home. My sneakers squelched with each step. I thought about taking them off to wring out my socks, but I knew if I stopped, it might evoke conversation. And that was something I refused to do. So I ignored the squishing sound and continued trudging behind Edmund.

Every mile or so, Edmund would turn to offer me water from a canister he had attached at his side. I ignored him every time, keeping my eyes and ears on the creatures that scurried around us in the forest.

Black birds drifted in the clear sky above, scattering through the tops of the giant trees. The rushing sound of their wings drew my attention upward, instead of watching my step. And my shoe caught on the root of a tree, which sent me crashing to the ground. My right foot was still recovering from the fall in the forest at Scarlet Heights, and now with my aching left foot, it seemed I had a matching pair.

"Are you hurt?" Edmund stood over me in seconds, reaching down to help me back to my feet.

"I'm fine," I grumbled. His cool hand slipped around my arm, but I pushed it away. "I don't want your help."

"I wish you would let me help," he said. Something told me he wasn't just talking about helping me out of the mud. His sincere tone almost made me feel bad for my deliberate harshness towards him, but then I focused on the night before. The way he'd snapped at me—the rage in his eyes. I thought back to all of the times he had deceived me and wondered how many more times there were that I just didn't know about. That was all I needed to squash any feelings of guilt.

My knees shook when I rose out of the mud, but nothing was broken or injured badly, just a few scrapes on my palms and knees. Most of the scrapes were covered in mud, so I used the bottom of my tattered dress to clean them. It was the best I could do.

I picked up walking as if I had never stopped; walking past Edmund while his eyes still stared from underneath his mask. He didn't move at first, frozen for whatever reason, he looked so far from human.

"Well? Are you coming or what?" I blurted over my shoulder.

"You are still the most difficult creature I've ever known," he said. "Why must you insist on taking the weight of this world on your shoulders?"

This question seemed to end the silent war between us, at least for the moment. I had a yearning to respond.

"Someone has to. Someone has to stop this."

"That person needn't take on the world alone."

"Am I not the one that everyone is counting on? The 'chosen one'? You have no idea how it feels to know that the fate of this world rests on me."

"You shouldn't carry this burden alone. No one should."

"No one should, but I must. I have to. For my father—for this kingdom," I said. "I'm not even sure why I was chosen. I'm nothing special, you know? So, why me? How do I know that I won't fail like the female guardians before me?"

"You won't fail. You are stronger than you think, Clara."

"But how do I know that I won't fall into temptation? How do I know I won't turn when the time comes?"

"You won't."

"You certainly did," I said, speaking without thinking. My hands moved to my mouth as if I might stuff the words back in. But too late.

His chest rose with deep breaths, in and out, in and out. And then he spoke.

"When I was faced with temptation, I failed to be the man I should have been. I made the wrong choice. Lust consumed and crippled me," he said. "But that won't happen to you."

"What temptation led to your fall? What were you promised that would lead you to turn against everything you believed in, against your kingdom— your own people?"

"The strength of the fallen is to be able to see your deepest desires, to know what it would take to tempt you. I was promised love, and all I had to do in return was swear to rule a kingdom of his choice. Victor was very convincing, insisting that I had nothing to lose, only love and adoration to gain, that there were no strings, that I could have it all. A kingdom, a binding love with the girl of my choosing. He made it easy to say yes. He never mentioned the terms of the agreement, that our deal was for Everest," he said, pausing for a moment to redirect his gaze away from mine. "And I didn't know the danger I would put you in, for wanting you. He didn't inform me of his plans with you."

"But you never cared for me. You were there, that night. You were helping him storm the castle. I tried to escape, and you locked me away."

"They came at night. By the time I learned of his plans to storm Everest, the damage had already been done. When I reached the castle, everyone was either missing or dead, and you were hurt...He tried for your soul, but when that didn't work, he took your memories. He thought if you didn't know who you were, that you would eventually give in to his power, that you would give him your soul, your gift—that you would be his in every possible way. When I heard of his plan, all I could do was try to protect you from them, from Victor and Erik and their army of fallen. I locked you away for your own protection; you must know that I never wanted harm to come to you."

His eyes glanced to mine.

"When you threw yourself from the castle, when I thought you were dead..." His voice cracked. "That's when I knew I had become the enemy—it

70

was my fault that the kingdom was overthrown, and I had killed one of God's own angels. I had become one of them, the very people we were sworn to hate. I became the monster in the night. I fell into darkness, Clara."

"Angel?" I muttered, still not believing what I'd heard.

"As soon as I heard you were still alive, I became obsessed with finding you. I sent out every fleet and demanded they bring me all girls within the southern forest of pine light. That is why the pirates captured you and brought you to me. And when I saw you, when you said your name and looked right into my eyes...I wanted nothing more than to have you forever, but I knew you would never love the monster I'd become. That is why I altered your perception. I knew you had loved Finn, so I tried to become what your heart wanted." His voice lowered. "I tried to be him."

"If you cared for me, why did you arrange for me to be near Victor? Why was he at the masquerade?"

"I'm not proud of what I've done," he said. "Victor was the only one who could make you mine. Make you my queen. I was meant to be your turn to evil. All I had to do was make you desire evil, to alter your perception and how you saw the world so that you would want to join the fallen. And I was going to turn you, until that night at the masquerade. That night changed me, Clara. You looked at me like you saw something good. You made me remember everything I loved about you, before I'd fallen. And how could I ever damn such a beautiful creature? I couldn't. That look made me want to be a better man, for you. I wanted to save you all over again."

"But that night, I overheard you. You said you would turn me."

"Those were only words. I had to tell Victor what he wanted to hear."

"So how do I know that your words are true now? How can I believe that any of this is true?"

"I know I have become an evil man, a damned man. I know I'm marked fallen. There's no saving me, but that doesn't mean I can't try for redemption—for good, that I can't want to save you. I have no reason to lie to you now, no ulterior motive other than to protect you and to try to piece together what is left of this kingdom," he said. "Saving you is the only thing that will bring me peace for all the wrong I have done. That is my truth."

His eyes held a deep and undeniable honesty. He felt guilty for his wrongs! The beast had a soul after all. I looked away, not knowing how to respond and focused instead on putting one foot in front of the other. Behind me, Edmund resumed walking as well.

I didn't know what to think of him. I was conflicted by what I thought I should be feeling and what I actually felt when I looked at him. Had he been telling the truth? Was it true that he longed for redemption? My brain tried to process everything he had told me. It was hard to hear the past from his perspective. To hear his struggle with evil, to know that it had gotten the best of him. It made the danger feel much more real. I had managed to escape it before, but could I again? All these new details mixing with my former knowledge created an overload of thoughts rambling in my head. Why was clarity such a fleeting concept?

"Have I frightened you?" Edmund asked after a few minutes had passed.

"It's a lot to process. But so is everything else." I awkwardly cleared my throat to signal I was finished with the subject. "Can you tell me more about where we are going?"

"We seek knowledge from the garden."

"The garden?"

He nodded. "Do you mind if I tell you a story? I believe it is the best way for you to…comprehend our destination."

"Okay, then. Tell me your story." I said, slowing my pace as I neared a fallen tree blocking our path.

Edmund was quick to dart to my side, offering a steady arm as I clumsily tried to climb over the decomposing trunk. This time, I accepted his help.

As soon as we both landed on the other side of the tree, the story began.

"To understand our quest, you must understand the history of this world. You see, at the birth of this world, there was a tree that sprouted before all other trees, absorbing all knowledge as its branches filled the sky. A sacred and beautiful garden grew around it, filled with nothing but good. The fruit of this garden was to go untouched by man; it was meant to remain a sacred place," he said. "But one day a beautiful woman entered the garden. Her cheeks were rosy, and her hair was red like fire. She'd been enticed by the beauty and the fruit of the garden, drawn to it by a voice in her head. The voice was like a mist around her, following her everywhere, calling to her by name, whispering of the fruit's power to give immortality. *Sienna, Sienna, beautiful Sienna. You can be a god*, the voice said."

I had heard a similar story before, told to me by my parents and grandparents, the story of light and darkness. Only Edmund told it with greater detail. His description of the beautiful woman led me to believe that this might be the redhead who had attacked me in Coushatta—the same one in Hades.

"Whose voice was it?" I wanted to know. "Who called to her?"

"It was Victor."

I nodded, and then gestured for him to continue the story.

"The woman was seduced by this desire for immortality. She longed for it. The day that she finally entered the garden, the voice appeared in human form, convincing her to follow him in. It was that day that she plucked a ripe apple from the tree and took a bite. *We can live like gods*, she repeated to him."

"What happened next?"

"After she'd devoured the fruit, the skies darkened, the earth shook, and the garden turned against them, forcing them out. God expelled her for disobeying, for eating the forbidden fruit. Both Victor and the woman were exiled to the Devil's Backbone—the land of Hades. And the garden disappeared."

"So how do you know where it is if it disappeared?"

"A few maps were left behind for the guardians." He held out a small scroll, carefully rolling an inch of parchment from the casing until latitude and longitude were visible. "Guardians are the only ones allowed passage into the garden—and only to seek knowledge from the tree."

"What does this have to do with me?"

"Everything. The very moment sin was brought into this world, a baby girl was born. She cried because she knew she was born into a sinful place. Her cries reminded God that there was still good left in this world, so he gave the baby the gift to destroy evil. The first female guardian. That is where it all began."

"And what of this tree?" I questioned. "Why are we searching for it?"

"The tree contains all knowledge of the past, present, and future, and it reveals this knowledge to those who are worthy of it. If we can make it through the garden to the tree, it will reveal the prophecy to you."

"Okay," I said. "Then I'm in."

A strong gust of wind blew past us, smelling sweet and clean, like honey and fruit, or roses after a fresh rain. But there were no honeycombs, fruit trees, or roses in sight.

"See that." Edmund pointed to the ground slightly ahead of us. It was less green, and random bits of rock were scattered through the grass. I didn't see any moss either, and the ground felt suddenly harder under my feet.

"Yeah."

"We're getting close," he said.

We continued on through the forest. I walked next to him now, sharing the remainder of the water he had left in his canister. After taking the last sip, I regretted not drinking any before.

We finally came to a place where the trees stopped and the lush grass gave way completely to dry, cracked earth that stretched for miles to the base of a mountain, but oddly enough, the sweet smells from before were stronger here, as if they were right under our noses.

Two golden statues appeared to guard the line between grass and rock. Each statue stood a good eight feet high, with four faces glaring in different directions. The face of a lion glared to the right, an ox to the left, and the face of a man and eagle faced forward. Both statues had two sets of wings, the hands of a man, and the feet of a calf. I had never seen anything like it. It was awe-inspiring and in-timidating at the same time.

"What are these?"

"Cherubs. They guard the entrance and the exit of the garden."

"There's nothing but rock here." I waved a hand toward the dusty ground that stretched ahead to the mountain in the distance. "Is this all that's left of the garden?"

He smiled slightly as he faced me. "That is what we are meant to think. Place your sword upon the cherub's hands."

I pulled my sword from its resting place and stepped up to one of the tall statues. I carefully lifted the blade and laid it across its outstretched hands.

As soon as the steel touched the one statue, all four heads of both creatures became animated with life and turned to face me. The lion roared, the ox snorted, and the eagle screeched.

"Who are you?" questioned one of the heads; the deep, metallic voice came from the human head to my right. I couldn't believe what I was seeing.

"I...I am Clarabella Calahan."

"Yes, yes we know your name," stated the human head of the cherub to my left in an identical voice to the first. "But who *are* you?"

"I am a guardian."

"Yes, yes. Precisely. It has been over five hundred years since we spoke to the last female guardian," he said. "Do you know why you are here, guardian?"

"Well, I'm not exactly certain." I pointed to Edmund. "He brought me here."

Edmund approached the creatures, not intimidated in the least. "Humble cherubs, she seeks knowledge from the tree."

"Very well. We cannot deny the female guardian her right to passage, but we must warn you that the garden can be a treacherous place for those who least expect it."

Edmund nodded. "That is why I ask that I may be her guide through the garden, to serve as her protector against what lurks inside."

"A strange request. It is not often one wishes to see to another's safe passage," said one cherub as the lion's head yawned. "We sense you are also of guardian blood."

The other chimed in, "Very noble, very noble indeed. I don't see why it should not be allowed."

"Neither do I," said the other.

And in perfect unison they said, "Your request is granted." The cherub to the right looked in my direction, and then added, "Take your sword, brave guardian. It is key to unlocking all knowledge."

"Do not be tempted to taste the fruit or drink the water from the garden," said the other. "We wish you well. God be with you both."

The arms of the statues stretched out to meet each other, forming an arch between them.

As soon as their fingers touched, their bodies turned back to gold, and a wooden door with a round iron handle appeared between them.

"Stay focused," Edmund said, grabbing for the handle to the gate. "And everything will be alright."

The door swung open and a single butterfly escaped.

6

GARDEN OF GOOD AND EVIL

FRUIT TREES WERE EVERYWHERE—APPLES, ORANGES, PLUMS, bananas, mangos, cherries—every fruit imaginable, and every one was ripe. Bright wildflowers bloomed at our feet, with petals of vivid colors I had never seen in the wild. Berries grew at the base of every tree. Every inch of the garden was lush and abundant with life, and the air smelled good enough to eat.

There was a loud slam behind us, drawing my immediate attention back to the gate.

"Edmund, the door!"

The gateway was gone. The cherubs and the wooden gate had disappeared completely. And now we were surrounded by the surreal landscape of the garden.

My heart thudded with panic. How would we get out? I had assumed our exit would be the same as our entry—one path in and one path out. Edmund had said the cherubs guarded them both. Now that the door was closed, would we be trapped in here forever?

"Do not let it worry you. If we make it to our destination, our exit will present itself," he said calmly. "Come on. It is important we spend as little time in here as possible."

If we make it to our destination? *If* was not a word that should be spoken. I started moving, allowing my eyes to take in more of the lush garden. The place looked harmless enough, and it was certainly the closest thing I'd ever seen to heaven, so why did it feel so treacherous?

"Edmund, what exactly did you mean by serving as my 'protector'? What is it that I need protection from?"

Before he could answer, I heard a shuffle of feet coming from my right. When I turned to look, I saw a figure leaning against a pink cherry tree. A bearded man dressed in noticeably worn clothes picked a handful of cherries and began tossing them into his mouth, two and sometimes three at a time.

"Come, over here," he cried in a rusty but strangely persuasive voice. How he was able to sound so beguiling with a mouthful of fruit, I'll never know. I was instantly drawn toward the tree. I wanted cherries from *that* tree, and I wanted them now.

I took a few steps toward the man before Edmund's hand jerked me back. The unexpected jolt left me shaken.

"What was that for?" I blurted.

"We stay true to the path," he said quickly. "Don't let them distract you."

"*Them*? How many others are here?"

"Keep moving," he said urgently. Apparently he saw something that I didn't, but I obeyed and actually picked up my pace a little. "We are not the first to cross beyond the threshold. In the past, many guardians have crossed over seeking wisdom from this place. Many failed to distance themselves from its rich bounty."

I didn't like where this was going, but I gestured for him to keep explaining as we quickly strode away from the old man.

"One bite of the garden's fruit, and you will become immortal. That is tempting for any man. But immortality comes with a price. Once you're immortal, the garden's fruit will no longer satisfy your hunger, its stream no longer quench your thirst. You are forced to wander about this place, hungry and thirsty for all eternity. Once you've tasted fruit from the garden, you can never leave."

"But aren't the guardians supposed to be on our side?"

"After an eternity of being cursed with hunger, thirst, and regret, they give in to madness. They are no longer on anyone's side. The only joy they can find is in causing the downfall of others. If they cannot coerce you into taking a bite, they might attack," he said. "That is why the cherubs allowed me to come with you. To protect you from them."

I heard another creepy voice coming from the distance, attempting to lure us into the shade of an apple tree. "You're hungry," the voice said. "Why don't you try an apple? It is very ripe…melts in your mouth."

"Don't even look at them," Edmund commanded. His words were beginning to make me nervous.

"Edmund, I can feel the desire pulling at me. Do you mind if I hold on to you?"

His arm extended, allowing just enough room for mine to wrap around it.

"Let's walk a little faster, shall we?"

As we picked up our pace, I became readily aware that Edmund was as worried as I was about succumbing to the fruit's temptation. And what if one of the former guardians tried to attack us? Were our swords of any use against them? This plan of journeying through the garden didn't appear to be well thought out.

"Once we make it to the rock, it is a straight climb from there. They are not allowed to go near the tree, so we will be safe on the mountain."

At least there was *some* good news.

I swallowed back pulses of hunger, walking in step with Edmund to make sure I didn't slow our brisk pace.

Hummingbirds streaked low overhead, searching for their next nectar-filled flower. I wondered if the garden had the same effect on them—cursing them with an eternity of thirst and hunger. I came to the conclusion that it didn't seem fair for an animal to be punished for the sins of man. Especially since the garden had never been off limits to them. If my conclusion was correct, then this garden was their haven of abundance.

Out of my peripheral vision, I started to notice more and more figures revealing themselves. We were outnumbered some twenty to one. Their momentary compliance with our desire to be left alone made me even more anxious. What were they waiting for?

"Why are they letting us through?"

"I'm not certain," Edmund replied, drawing my arm closer to his body.

Even hidden under his mask, his face betrayed his worry. Every time his eyebrows furrowed, the top of his mask would lower slightly, exposing tiny wrinkles on his forehead. Those wrinkles had been visible since we stepped into the garden.

Suddenly the tops of the trees before of us began to shake. This was something I'd seen happen in the forests of Everest when monkeys would swing from branch to branch. But these couldn't be monkeys. The trees were shaking entirely too much. There was something bigger hiding in their branches.

We veered to the left, taking a path through a thick row of peach trees. My arm slipped from Edmund's as we broke into a run, but he quickly grabbed my hand to pull me along. The movement of the trees now chased us from behind and grew more violent as it came closer and closer to us. Were these mad gorillas or something else? Could we outrun them? I was already beginning to feel winded. I reminded myself to inhale and exhale from my stomach, to stop breathing through my nose and breathe with my mouth. We darted in and out of the path, trying to lose the mysterious creatures, with no luck.

The trees rattled to our right and left, passing us to get in the lead once more. And then the two creatures revealed themselves, flying from the trees to land only yards ahead of us.

At first glance, they appeared to be something like bears. They walked straight for us, their long furry arms held out, reaching. But then I realized they weren't bears at all. They were people—a man and a woman, to be exact. They were dressed in bearskins, and their hands and faces were smudged with mud. Both had the craziest looks in their eyes.

The man spoke first. "Those who do not join us..."

"...feed us!" The woman giggled.

"Cannibals," I whispered. *They are absolutely mad.*

"The girl appears to understand," said the man in a quirky tone. "I think I'll have to kill her first!"

Edmund released my hand and pushed me behind him to stand before our predators alone.

"You will have to come through me first." His voice came out as a growl.

It was nice to see his rage unleashed on someone other than myself. He'd snapped at me so many times before, but witnessing now the full, blazing heat of his fierce energy, I realized that those times he'd lashed out at me seemed like politeness in comparison. I imagined it would be even more intense if he were free of his mask, if his face was exposed to reveal what had to be a terrifying expression.

He drew the sword from his leather belt, gripping the hilt with both hands.

The two crazies reached behind their backs, drawing their own blades.

I knew that Edmund had every intention of fighting them alone and that he would probably be furious if I jumped in to help, but I was not going to sit back and watch him fight them both. I readied my sword just as they made their first move.

The man struck first, leaping forward like a bobcat toward Edmund. Edmund caught his steel, striking it so hard that the man staggered backward into his crazy fur-wearing partner, who had been playfully twirling her sword behind him.

"That's all you've got?" shouted the man through laughter.

The crazy woman stepped forward with the man this time, waving her sword in the air between us.

I repositioned myself beside Edmund.

"Stay back," he said to me.

Both crazies lunged, giving me no other choice but to stand my ground and counter. The sound of steel against steel interrupted the birdsong that had filled the garden before. Edmund and I fought side by side, advancing in the first few minutes of the attack. But then the crazy woman was gaining the advantage—she was meeting my blade before I could even get it high into the air. Had my moves become predictable? I tried striking from every angle, lunging in quick intervals; I just couldn't get my blade ahead of hers.

Before I knew it, I found myself blocking more and losing ground. Out of the corner of my eye I saw Edmund turn. I couldn't see his eyes from where I stood, but I imagined he was concerned over my switch from offense to defense.

His blade moved faster, pushing the wild man back. The steel of his blade sliced once against the man's chest, cutting the strap that held the bearskin to his back. The man's fur coat dropped, and Edmund side-kicked the same area he had wounded. Down the man went, dropping his sword and flailing backward into a tree. Edmund was quick to reach him, sending the end of his blade straight through the man's throat. It was brutal.

It's hard to account for what happened next, because it happened so fast, but suddenly Edmund was standing behind the woman as her body dropped to the ground. My relief was mirrored in Edmund's eyes as our gazes met.

I let the tip of my sword drop to the ground, my arms aching and my breathing shallow. "I don't know what it was, but I couldn't get my blade ahead of hers."

"She was reading your mind, Clara. A telepathic."

"What?"

"Have you forgotten already?" he asked, teasingly. Hearing his lighter tone seemed so out of place after the attack, but automatically lifted the heavy mood. "Only guardians have ever entered the garden. Those who you see now are the guardians who never made it back out."

This limp body before me had been like me once? A female guardian with the burden to kill the fallen. And she had failed. I wondered if this crazy woman had any recollection of who she had been. I wondered what century she had been from. I wondered what change her failure had brought in the lost world.

Edmund poked her body with the toe of his boot to see if she was going to get back up. She didn't.

"Hurry," he said. "They will heal soon."

"They look pretty dead to me."

"They are immortals. They will heal," he said with certainty.

The garden was much quieter when we picked up the trail. Immortals were still watching us from behind trees, lurking in bushes, but no more approached us. I hoped this was a sign that we were nearing the mountain.

After cutting through a few more rows of apple trees, an assortment of cherry trees, grape vines, and banana trees, we came to the bottom of the mountain.

We didn't hesitate to start our climb.

At first it was more like walking up a rocky hill, but after a few minutes, it increased to a much steeper incline.

"Please tell me," I paused to exhale, "...that we're almost there."

"Just a little further, Clarabella." He smiled encouragingly back at me.

My mouth became very dry, very fast. "We're completely out of water, aren't we?"

"I'm afraid so."

Great, I thought. We had no idea how much longer we would be stuck in the garden, and we had no food or water. Oh, and as an added bonus, we were surrounded by the most tempting fruit and water of all time, which we were unable to touch without damning ourselves to eternal life in a garden full of crazy people. *Perfect.*

The trail veered into a switchback up the mountain face as the incline became too steep to climb without holding on. At this point, we found there were manmade steps dug into it, for which I was grateful.

We climbed on.

One hundred and fifty-five steps later (I counted), we came to the very top.

The glowing silhouette of a tree stood before us, with warm rays of sun pouring through its full branches. The tree was alone on top of that mountain, silently overlooking the beauty of the garden below. All traces of the bitter immortals had vanished now, hidden under the colorful canopy of fruit trees.

"We made it."

"Almost. Let's see your sword," he said, pointing to my leather belt that held it snuggly to my side.

I stretched the heavy sword out in front of me and positioned myself in front of the tree. Edmund stepped up behind me, wrapping his arms around me so that we both held the hilt of the sword. I felt his weight push forward, leading the blade to the trunk of the tree. I leaned with his encouragement.

The tip of steel sliced into the bark of the tree with ease. Edmund continued to push me forward as the blade sank deeper into the trunk.

"Hold on tightly," he whispered.

Suddenly, the blade seemed to anchor as a wind began to whip around us. The branches of the tree shook vigorously in the gusts, showering us with hundreds of leaves. The sun slid behind an enormous cloud, shadowing all the land around us. And then the tree began to distort. I blinked heavily, watching the bark crack away from its trunk and its green leaves explode into thin air, before it was gone. The entire tree—gone. Edmund held me tightly as we slid away from the light, into sultry nothingness. The wind ceased to exist, and its loud roar was replaced with an echoing crackle. Then light appeared.

It took a moment for my eyes to adjust before realizing that walls of sandstone surrounded us like a tomb, and the light was coming from two flaming swords held by stone arms extending from the wall. *Where are we? Another time? Another place?*

I took in our new surroundings. My own sword, which our hands still clung to, now protruded straight from sandstone. That explained our anchor. Edmund's hands slid from mine, allowing me to release my grasp on the hilt. I massaged my fingers for a second while my eyes continued to adjust to the dull light.

The two fiery swords reaching out from the wall of the cave illuminated red markings along the rough surface of the stone.

"What is this place?" I finally asked out loud.

"This is the place that holds the prophecy. This is the knowledge the tree offers you. The prophecy has been nothing more than a legend to most, considered to be merely myth. Only the female guardians who have come before you have stood on this ground, because only a guardian, the holder of this sword can enter the threshold."

"You forget to mention how every female guardian before me has failed."

"Yes." His voice was hollow. "But where they failed, you will succeed."

So this was it—the truth to my purpose. My destiny, written in stone. Literally. I looked at the words carved into the wall—Latin, as I had expected. My mind felt especially clear here, in this strange limbo, and the translation flowed more easily than ever before. How many centuries of women had stood right where I was to read this for the first time? If I failed, just as they had, then I wouldn't be the last one. I shuddered at the thought and then began to read the prophecy aloud.

Guardian, oh guardian, here is your task:
Rid this world of evil at last.

Righteous men bleed for all that is right,
Seeking their liberty from the dark night.

Weak men fall to restless walls of fire,
Marked with their sins of lust, greed, and desire.

Blood flows, yet evil continues to spread,
For it is the chosen whose blood must be shed.

Only then shall the righteous win this fight,
Filling a world of darkness with His light.

Guardian, oh guardian, that comes to pass
You are the one who must act fast.

The lust of man has marked you slaved;
Through grace alone can this world be save.

Another shiver ran down my spine, as I tried to memorize each phrase before me. I had only read through the prophecy three times, when the ground under our feet began to shake.

"Our time is up, Clara. We found what we were looking for, now we must leave," Edmund said, pulling me toward him.

"But I don't understand the prophecy...I need more time."

A strange wind began to flood the tomb, howling like a pack of wolves.

"You will. We must go, Clara!"

Edmund wrapped his body around mine, guiding both of our hands to the hilt that still projected from the wall of sandstone.

As we struggled to pull the sword from the wall, the wind grew stronger, the howls, louder. The intense sound turned quickly to voices, dozens of voices whispering in the wind. I could hear them clearly, as if they were all around. *For no one chooses the chosen—it is the chosen that choose themselves,* the voices said. They grew louder, speaking the words like a chant. *For no one chooses the chosen—it is the chosen that choose themselves,* they repeated.

The stone before us cracked, and the light of day seeped into the darkness. I had to squint to keep my eyes open against the piercing brightness. We continued to pull the sword, watching as the light engulfed the entire wall. The wind and voices were strongest at this point, whipping through our clothes, tangling my hair. Then, just as the tip of the sword pulled free, the wind and voices ceased to exist; the bright light dulled and revealed the two cherubs that had greeted us at the entrance of the garden.

I turned my head, looking in every direction. Bright green grass grew under my feet; a setting sun lay in the western sky. Behind us was the unmistakable marshy forest, and before us, the golden cherubs guarding miles and miles of stone and mountain. We had ended where we began, as if nothing had happened.

Edmund's arms were still tightly wrapped around me; his hands were still on mine as they gripped the sword. We were breathing together, long steady breaths. I wondered if his mind was racing as much as mine.

"What happened? We were there, in the garden—the mountain, the tree, and the prophecy...you saw it too, right?"

"Yes, I was there." Edmund said, loosening his grip from around me as he stepped away. It felt too soon for him to let go, but I wasn't sure why.

"And the voices? Did you hear the voices?"

"I heard them, too."

"So it was real?"

"It was very real, Clara."

I frowned, piecing it all together. The whole experience had happened so quickly, seemed too strange, too surreal, almost like a dream.

"So how did we get back here? It's like we never left."

"That is how the garden works," he said. "You were worthy of the message it had to offer, you passed the test, and so we were given an exit."

"But what does it all mean?" I shifted my weight uncomfortably, worried that I'd learned nothing from the journey. I felt fatigue starting to settle in with my confusion.

"It is said that the tree offers different knowledge to every guardian, that each one is given a special message, and that it's up to that guardian to decipher the meaning behind it. In time, you will understand it. Just like everything else."

Edmund seemed so calm as he spoke, so certain that I would figure out the riddle behind the words given to me by the tree. I had hoped it would be written plainly. I had wanted precise instructions; I had wanted to know exactly what needed to be done to end all of this. Instead, it left me with more questions. More uncertainty.

I nodded, looking up at the grand cherubs, who appeared, somehow, even more majestic than before. As my eyes took in the scene one last time, there was one phrase going through my mind—one phrase I did understand.

Blood flows, yet evil continues to spread, I thought. *For it is the chosen whose blood must be shed.*

7

BEHIND THE MASK

THE SKIES WERE TURNING GREY WHEN WE STARTED BACK TO camp, and the grey swiftly darkened to an endless black filled with millions of stars.

As the forest turned to colors that only a blue moon could provide, it occurred to me for the first time that long day that Edmund and I were alone—completely alone, with only the dark silhouettes of trees for company. The night pushed us together as it deepened. We had been alone the entire day, and it hadn't bothered me. I hadn't thought about it in the least. So why now? I couldn't put my finger on it. There was a strange awkwardness when I thought about it. I wasn't scared of him anymore, so that couldn't be it. He wasn't using any mind tricks on me anymore. Or threatening me. There were no ill words or talk of the past. We were just walking through the woods, side by side. And he was being nice.

Then I realized what it was.

I was actually comforted that he was with me and that I wasn't wandering around this world by myself. Relieved, even. It was a welcome relief to have someone on my team, someone to look out for me. A friend—almost, I think.

Edmund fidgeted with his vest pocket, pulling out the small scroll he'd shown me earlier in the day.

He rolled it out and studied it for a moment, tracing a new path with his fingers.

"There seems to be a creek, just north of our initial path. We'll camp there for the night," he said, "and head back to the lake at dawn."

"Any place with water will suit me fine," I croaked. "My mouth tastes like chalk."

A low chuckle vibrated from his chest. "Mine, too."

The next half an hour was excruciating. We both walked in silence, hoping to conserve what little saliva there was left in our mouths. I didn't know my tongue could get that dry. So, when we heard the soft trickle of water, we took off sprinting toward it, unloading everything we carried in the process.

At the water's edge, I crashed to my knees, dunking my entire face into the fresh water, drawing in as much of the creek as I could in one breath. Edmund knelt next to me doing the same. Before long, we were both waist deep in water, trying to soak in every bit of it.

Edmund's wet hair was slicked away from the edges of his mask. I hoped that being so wet, it might slip, that I'd finally get to stand face to face with this mysterious man.

"What's it like," I questioned, touching my own face, "to be behind such a mask?"

"Do you really wish to know?"

"Yes, I do. I want to know how it feels to be you...I want to understand you."

"Close your eyes," he instructed. His hands lightly touched my shoulders, turning my back to him. I stood quietly, listening hard to the sound of

movement behind me, curiously and anxiously awaiting his next move.

Suddenly, his hand reached around me to cradle
my chin, and a blanket of cold slid over my face.
Cold, smooth, wet. It wrapped around my temples,
gripping my entire forehead. The porcelain fit hard
against the bridge of my nose and cheeks. It rubbed
uncomfortably against my skin, but I refrained from
flinching. I wanted to know how he felt every day.

Edmund's hands moved away from the mask
and back to my shoulders. He was hiding behind me,
no doubt.

"Tell me what you feel."

I blinked open my eyes to peer through the slits
in the mask. The world looked different, somehow.
Further away. Disconnected. I noticed my breathing
quicken.

"I feel…trapped," I responded. "Separated from
the forest and from this water. I feel separated from
you."

"There is your answer."

His hands swiftly freed my face from the mask,
and before I'd turned around, the mask was back
imprisoning his.

I found myself staring hard at him again, taking
in every detail of the slanted lines of the cheeks, the
straight line of the nose, the carved expression of the
porcelain eyebrows. It was hard to believe how chas-
tising something so beautiful could be.

His eyes watched mine. I followed the lines of
the porcelain again until it met with his skin. The
broadness of his own chin was sculpted just as flaw-
lessly as the mask above it. His perfectly curved lips

were just slightly open, daring me to stare. It seemed as though the mask wore him as much as he wore it. They were one. Both smooth, pale, frozen perfect.

Something stirred in my chest. An emotion I couldn't quite place. For a moment I thought we were drifting together in the water; he was getting closer to me, at least. I felt disoriented, but not how I'd been before. It wasn't any kind of enchantment; I'd grown aware of how that felt, and this was different. It was more of an unsettling connection. I briefly felt his pain, his longing to be a part of a world he had disconnected himself from. He'd been punishing himself all along for all of the damage he'd caused in this world. His guilt haunted and crippled him. The mask was his way of concealing his shame. I understood, now.

He was the first to break his gaze away. "I should gather logs for a fire," he stated. "It will get cold through the night. You shouldn't sleep in damp clothes."

He offered his hand, escorting me out of the water. I stepped over to the oak that overlooked us and began to shuffle out of my sneakers.

"Wait here," he said. "I'll return shortly."

I threw my weight down into the soft green earth and pushed my sore back against the trunk of the oak. The sudden pressure felt good against my lower back. All the walking and climbing had strained several muscles that I hadn't used in a long time. Edmund returned shortly with three logs cradled in his right arm and a long, narrow branch in his left hand. The branch appeared to be a yard or so long and only a couple of inches wide, not really large enough to aid in the construction of a fire.

He dropped the branch, and then quickly got to work on the fire.

As the blaze took hold of the wood, he brought out a short dagger and chipped away at the end of the branch until it formed a sharp point.

"I thought you might be hungry," he said. "And it seems there are plenty of fish in the creek."

I smiled. "Fish sounds amazing right now." I pushed up from the tree and gradually walked to him as he put his knife away. "Can I help?"

"You should rest."

"So should you," I retorted. "Let me help."

His lips curved upwards as he motioned for me to follow him. We both waded into the water until we were knee deep.

"You forgot your spear," I said, now noticing he was without it.

"That's for cooking. We catch them with our hands."

This was going to be a first. With my parents, I'd done plenty of fishing with lines and nets. Never with my hands.

The moon spread a soft light through the water, showcasing several fish swimming about. He walked among them, slipping between their swimming bodies as if he were one with the current. I lagged behind, failing miserably at going unnoticed. The fish scattered.

"Sorry," I whispered.

He reached back and grabbed my hand, pulling me to waist-deep water.

"It's like a dance," he said. His arms wrapped around my waist and swung me around in front of him. "Step with me."

He kept his arms around my waist and instructed me to put my feet on top of his. After I was balanced with my back against his chest, he lifted his right foot from the creek bottom, and then gracefully glided us forward. His feet slid back and forth in a slow tempo, pausing in intervals.

"If you move to the music, you won't disturb them."

"Music?"

"Listen hard, it's there." He paused in the water for a moment, keeping us perfectly still in the moving current around us. "Can you hear it?"

I strained, searching for notes, for distinct interludes or harmonies supposedly hidden around us. I couldn't hear anything. Edmund began to hum a melody very softly in my ear. It fit the movements of his dance. The music of the forest. The water that rolled over the rocks produced the rhythm, and the wind through the trees played intervals of notes.

"I can hear it now." I was amazed that I'd lived my life never knowing there'd been an orchestra playing around me all along. I found myself moving my arms in the water, moving with the song, with the current.

"Good," he whispered. "Now look down."

There were fish swimming all around us now, even a few floating in place. We had become a part of the creek, the fish seeing us as just another inanimate object that the water flowed around.

Edmund's hands found mine, slowly guiding them deeper in the water. Our backs were arched now, our faces only inches from the surface. It was easy to see the bodies of the fish; I had my eye on one that had been swimming around my knees.

"Almost...almost..." Edmund muttered, positioning our hands to float toward the fish. "Now."

He forced our hands together quickly, looping our fingers around our dinner. As I pulled the struggling fish from the water, he released my hands so that I could take it to shore.

He followed behind with another fish already flapping in his hand.

In minutes he had them on the spear and hanging over the fire.

"Do you believe there is redemption for any man who longs for it?" he asked as he rotated the spear, staring moodily into the flames.

As I looked at him, I could no longer see the man who aided in the destruction of a kingdom. I saw a man who was full of regret—a man drowning in his own self-loathing. How could I condemn a man who desired redemption? Isn't it true that all people sin? That we all must desire redemption in order to be saved from our own evil? If that were true, then how could I look at him and say that he could not be redeemed—that he was doomed for all eternity? It was the guardian way to forgive.

"I believe it can be found by any man who searches for it."

I could tell by his expression that my words had pleased him. I tried to back up, to pull away from the emotion that was overtaking me, but it was useless. The sincerity of his question had melted my heart.

"There's hope for you yet, Edmund."

"Hope," he whispered, smiling at the very word.

Soon the fish were fully cooked and ready to eat. We both devoured our portions, speaking only briefly to ask the other how theirs tasted. Before long, we were back down by the water, washing down our meal with its cool freshness.

Edmund started back to the fire while I rinsed my hands and face. He'd already begun to assemble a tent, using the woolen blanket from my satchel and the limb of the oak I'd rested against. It was a higher branch, making a taller shelter. I walked back to the fire just as he secured the bottom corners of the tent with four large creek stones. Once he finished he stood and turned toward me.

"Your satchel is inside. You should find the other blanket in there as well." He started to unbutton his vest as he walked closer to the fire. "We should dry our clothes. You can leave yours outside the tent. I'll collect them and sit by the fire while they dry."

I raised a teasing eyebrow in response.

Edmund chuckled for a moment, realizing how his request must have sounded. "Don't worry, they will be by your tent, waiting for you in the morning."

"Okay," I agreed. "Thanks for the tent, by the way."

"It was my pleasure." He took a slow breath, seemingly composing himself. He started to take a few steps in my direction, but then stopped.

"Clara, there was something I wanted to tell you."

"Yes?" I gave him my full attention. The truth was, I really wanted to talk to him. I wanted him to tell me all his secrets, all his thoughts. I wanted to understand everything that had happened before, in that time that felt so long ago. It seemed he had a lot to tell and that he needed me to listen.

He studied my face, as if he were anticipating a reaction. In the silence, I concentrated on the only part of his face visible to me, waiting for his pale lips to move—waiting to hear what they had to say. Finally they parted.

"I wanted to tell you goodnight," he said, clearing his throat. "So—umm, goodnight, Clara. Sleep well."

He turned, as I responded with a soft echo of his goodnight. Disappointment fell over me, leaving me with a sharp desire to run to him—to plead with him to tell me the real thoughts that had been on his mind, but instead I crawled into the waiting darkness of the tent. I knew there was more he had to say, there just had to be. I had felt something there in the silence, something lingering in the awkwardness, but what was it?

I carefully removed my damp dress, tossing it outside my tent, and then replaced it with the clean golden blanket from the satchel. I heard movement outside as Edmund collected my dress. It was all I could do not to cry out to him. Instead, I tucked my blanket tightly under my arms, feeling somewhat more comfortable, and stretched out under the canopy.

When we were younger, Edmund had always looked out for me. My mother believed that the two of us would eventually marry. The idea even pleased the Senate. Finding suitable marriage prospects was one of their many functions. Especially when it came to guardians. Though arranged marriages were not exactly their style, certain relationships would be encouraged, and some were downright forbidden. I found it odd that the idea was still clear in my memory. Why had we been such a perfect match back then? And why was I thinking about this right now?

Did Edmund remember? My thoughts kept straying back to the idea that the Senate's past encouragement would have made sense. We had both been children of great guardian knights. We both were said to have a great destiny entwined into one. I didn't know what that meant then, and I sure didn't know what it meant now.

My eyes were just drifting closed when I heard footsteps approaching my tent. I knew he was probably just coming to return my clothes, as promised, but I couldn't help hoping that he might have changed his mind. Maybe he was ready to talk.

When the footsteps came all the way to the mouth of the tent, I rolled over to sit up. "I was hoping you would come," I said, lifting my head to greet him.

I flushed with surprise.

A pair of angry green eyes briefly flashed over my blanket-wrapped body, then met my astonished gaze. "Sorry to disappoint."

"F-Finn," I stammered.

I had spent the last year dreaming of the moment he'd stand before me again. Finn! But now, as he glared down on me, my dream was shattered. I could only imagine what he thought of me now. How bad this must've looked. I wished I knew the right thing to say, how to explain everything, but my brain was useless. From his expression, I knew words wouldn't have helped anyway.

I got to my knees so that I was no longer straining my neck, but sat stiffly with the small woven blanket held even tighter around my body. I felt flushed with confusion, with dozens of questions running through my head.

"How did you...know I was here? Where is Edmund...?" I was having a difficult time focusing on what I wanted to ask.

"There was word that you had been drawn back into this world. We have been following your tracks for days," he said. "I feared you were held prisoner, but it seems you are here willingly. I misjudged you."

"It's not what it looks like," I said. "Did you hurt him?"

"Not yet," he said turning his back to me. "But the night is not over. Now, get dressed." He threw my own clothes at my lap and quickly marched away from the tent.

This was terrible. I was so happy to see Finn— but not like this! I'd pictured our reunion being much different, much sweeter—loving. I'd imagined he would throw his strong arms around me and twirl me from my feet. I thought I'd finally get to taste that sweet cinnamon of his kiss again. I had pictured so many different versions of our perfect meeting. But I never thought it would be anything like this.

My hands trembled while I slid back into my dress, still warm from the fire. *What will they do to Edmund?* There was no doubt that Finn was furious. I knew he already hated Edmund, for the same reasons I had, but my view had changed. Finn would never see Edmund the way I saw him now. He'd never give him a chance to explain. Edmund was no saint, but he certainly deserved the chance to explain himself.

I forced my soggy shoes on and sprinted from the tent. Soldiers were everywhere—around thirty altogether, invading our entire campsite. Four of them had Edmund in ropes, strategically knotting them so that he had no chance of escape.

Those four soldiers stood out from the others, wearing a special emblem on their navy uniforms. This emblem, a golden shield embroidered across the front of the uniform and its sleeves, was the emblem of the guard. These were a small group of soldiers dedicated to serving the Senate. They were much different than the guardian knights or the king's soldiers. The guard only took orders from the Senate; the king had no rule over them. The guard and the Senate were established long ago in order to protect the people if the reigning king happened to turn evil. They helped to see that our king enforced the laws of our kingdom.

My heart fell straight into my stomach. This was much worse than I initially thought. It wasn't just Finn I had to worry about. The Senate showed no mercy and listened to no one; the guard simply carried out their orders. Edmund would surely be brought straight to the Senate. And no one would listen to him; he'd be punished before ever speaking a word.

Kalani was here, too. She stood by the fire with the group of elders huddled around her. Had they betrayed Edmund? Led Finn and his men straight to us? I found myself angry with all of them, even Finn for bringing members of the guard. I stormed over to the fire, singling out Kalani.

"How could you lead them to us? Do you know what they'll do to Edmund?"

She looked distraught. "Kalani do no such thing. They find us. They find you."

"You had nothing to do with this?"

"No…no…" She shook her head, tears gathering in her eyes.

I heard Finn's voice interrupt. "She's telling the truth. If you want to be angry with someone, be angry with me. I did this. I'm the one raiding your fantasy."

"You don't understand, Finn."

"Well, make me understand, Clara. Tell me why I find you with our enemy. Tell me why you looked disappointed to see me. It is quite clear that I interrupted something between the two of you."

I felt sick to my stomach, dryness in my mouth.

"It's not like that. He and I…we're not…He's not who we thought, Finn."

"He's exactly who I thought."

"Edmund is different. He's changed."

"You talk as though he's found salvation. Men like Edmund do not change, Clara. They only fool you into thinking they have."

"Don't we believe that redemption comes for any man who longs for it, who desires it with all of his being?" I questioned. "To condemn him would be to contradict everything the guardians believe."

"He does not deserve redemption."

"You honestly don't think that...do you?" I asked.

His face showed no signs of mercy. Nothing but hate. I wanted to tell him to take it back, but I knew he never would.

"Where is your compassion?"

"He will not find any compassion from me. He has no soul." His voice was low, but stern. "We will take him back to the castle and let the Senate decide his fate. It is the code."

"But, Finn...please..."

"It is the code that binds us. If we don't honor it, then we are no better than our enemy."

"So that's it then? You're not going to listen to a word I have to say?"

"Not when it's about him. He will be punished, Clara. And there's nothing you can say that will change my mind. Death is certainly in his near future."

I almost couldn't breathe. How could I make Finn understand that he was making a mistake? We didn't have time for this. Edmund needed to be free. We both needed to be free so that we could help the people of Zy—so that we could find my father before it was too late.

I looked to Kalani for help. "Kalani, tell him. Tell Finn what you told me."

Her head drooped and slowly shook.

"Tell him how he helped you. Tell him…"

I saw her look up through the long lashes that shaded her caramel eyes. "He want this."

I rolled my eyes as I stormed off to the edge of the creek. The clouds above us began to release small drops of cool rain. It was fitting how it always rained at dramatic moments in my life. So cliché.

No one bothered me, but I caught Finn's eyes every so often. Probably checking to see that I hadn't run away. Or been kidnapped.

Though I was frustrated with him, Finn still looked as handsome and desirable as I remembered him. His hair had grown slightly longer, but it was still the same perfectly tousled, rich brown hair from before. His muscles seemed to have grown, too, not that he was scrawny before, but his boyish appearance had completely given way to full manhood. There was so much I'd wanted to say to him, things that had built up in my mind over the past year. Things I'd even practiced saying. But all of it would have to wait. The mood wasn't there. It hurt to be this close to him and to still feel so far away. It hurt to love him the way that I did and to be angry with him.

The clouds rumbled, bringing more rain. I forced myself to put my thoughts of Finn aside so that I could concentrate on the matter at hand. *Edmund*. I had to help him. There had to be some way to help him escape. All I had to do was sneak around after dark and cut the ropes. *Simple*, I thought. After he's loose, the two of us could run to the lake and swim with the current, let it take us away from here. Were the canoes still there? I didn't know what Edmund had planned to do before we were captured, but surely he'd had some type of plan. Maybe he had a ship waiting for us at the coast. It didn't really matter. I just needed to get him loose first. Then we could figure out how to get to Zy. The two of us, we could do this, I reassured myself.

I listened to the conversations coming from around the smoldering fire until I found Finn's distinct husky voice. I overheard him instruct his men that we would be staying here for the night and that we would leave at dawn. He planned to travel through the forest and meet with a ship at the coast. We would sail around the coast, directly to the castle—where the Senate would surely be waiting. I couldn't let this happen. If I was going to help Edmund, it had to be tonight. Our only hope for a successful escape would be to get ahead of the group, beat them out of the forest.

Tents began to go up behind me as men prepared to get their rest for the night. I was soaked to the bone by this point, but it didn't seem to matter since I'd be out in the rain again later. Finn broke away from his soldiers and started to walk to me. I made sure that my back was to him when he approached.

"You shouldn't be out in this rain," he said. "You'll catch cold."

His arm extended, holding a coat over my head.

"Please don't do this, Finn."

"Even if I believed you, I cannot let him go. The guard would never allow it."

"Maybe you could talk to them. You are king, after all. You have to have some say in the matter."

"They are bound by law to obey the Senate, not the king. All I can do is keep you from getting into trouble. If you continue with this, they will have no choice but to take you as well. The guard already questions your loyalty, Clara." He paused. "It was all I could do to convince them of your innocence, that you and the Zyons had been captured by Edmund."

"But that's not true!"

"Clara, Edmund is deceptive. And I won't let you fall into his web of lies, not again. He shall stand trial in front of the Senate. It is only fair."

"Fair? You know they will crucify him."

"They will judge him accordingly. I cannot help that he will be on trial for treason."

"So you won't even give him a chance?"

"He had his chance. Now it's time for him to pay for what he did with it."

I pushed away from the shelter of his coat, letting the rain beat down against my skin once more.

"I thought you of all people would listen, but I was wrong. Revenge is the only thing you can hear. You used to be a great man." My words were delivered through clenched teeth, each pulsing more anger through my body as it entered the air between us.

My feet started to shift, until they made their own decision to walk away.

"Clara…"

"Do not follow me," I hissed as I stormed away. My own demand for space felt strange and uncomfortable as I said it, but it was necessary. He left me no other choice. As much as I loved Finn and longed to be with him, I had to set those feelings aside and run away with Edmund. And I didn't have much time to orchestrate my plan. My eyes were down as I stomped past the remainder of soldiers outside their tents. Kalani was already tucked away nicely in a dry tent and so were the elders. I was glad that I wouldn't have to exchange glances with them right now. I was still angry that none of them stood up for Edmund.

I waited quietly inside my tent, watching as the rain pushed everyone inside their own. Finn stood by the water a good while after I'd left, frozen in the same spot that I'd left him, still staring down at the moving water. I felt guilty for how harsh I'd been, but I reminded myself that there was no other way. He wouldn't listen. There was nothing else I could do. When the clouds finally bottomed out, dropping sheets of hard rain, he took shelter in his tent.

Hours passed, filled with rolling thunder and flickers of lightning in the distant sky. The fire had long been out, and all was still among the tents. During a long boom of thunder, I rolled out from under the back of my shelter and sprinted around the campsite, until I came to the tree where Edmund was strapped in a standing position.

His eyes were closed, and his mask pointed to the ground when I reached him.

"Edmund, are you alright?" I whispered.

His head tilted slightly upward. I held his face for a moment, waiting for his eyes to focus. The soft lines of his lips moved just enough so that I knew he'd become alert.

"I'm getting you out of here."

"Are you trying to save my soul?" he asked, a small amount of hope in his voice, barely audible over the blustering of the storm.

"There's still good in you. I know there is. It doesn't have to be this way."

"I wish you were right."

"I have seen it. You have been trying to save me all along."

"That is not the good in me."

"Then what? If not good, what saved me that night in the castle? Why did you protect me from Victor? Why did you bring me here so that I could see the prophecy?"

"Because," he said softly. "I've loved you all along."

I stared blankly into the night, holding my breath.

"It does not matter now," he said finally. "In the end, you will have to choose. This is written—it's your destiny. So please, do not pretend to care about me. It will only hurt more in the end."

I stepped forward until I stood only inches from his drooping body. I tried to soak in the truth behind his words, but my emotions momentarily rejected it. Deep down I knew that he was right about my destiny, but I still hoped that I could write my own destiny—that I could change everything.

I cut the ropes binding his feet first, and then the ones tied so tightly around his bleeding wrists.

He staggered slowly toward me in the night, extending a hand to mine so that it slid threw my fingers. He pushed my hands behind my back softly and leaned closer to me. His face neared mine; his lips parted. I kept my eyes focused on his, immersed in the sadness behind them. Rain wrapped around us as I waited for his next move.

"I'm sorry," he whispered.

Before I had time to process these words, I felt my arms pull together. A damp rope wound around my wrists like a treacherous snake, locking them together.

"What are you doing?"

"Keeping you safe," he said. "Finn will protect you, at all costs. He will look after you now."

"Don't you dare do this to me. Untie me right now," I said sternly, still trying to keep my voice low. I wanted to scream at him, but I was too afraid that I would alert one of the soldiers.

Edmund replied by looping another rope around my legs.

"You cannot follow me. I understand what it is I am meant to do. This is my downfall. But you are meant for so much more," he said. "You will rise stronger than anyone ever dreamed."

I suddenly realized that this had been his plan all along. He'd wanted Finn and his soldiers to track us down. He wanted us to get caught—he never meant for me to go with him to Zy. How foolish of me to fall right into it.

"I know what you're doing, Edmund—and you just can't. You can't leave me here! And you certainly can't give your life for me. It's not right. I won't let you."

"You have no say in the matter. I'm going. This is the way I can love you. This is the only way I know how."

I knew he would no more listen to me than he would set me free. But I gave one last plea.

"Take me with you. Please. You know that it is my destiny to stop this. You've seen the prophecy just as I have. We both know that I must die to end the war. Why do you wish to fight what is already written?"

"Because there has to be another way. And I won't let you stop me from finding it." His fingers grazed my cheek, pushing a stray strand of wet hair away. "Let me show you I can be a better man."

"Please—"

His fingers silenced my words, lingering on my mouth. "Stay safe, Clarabella," he said, pressing his cool lips to my cheek. "I will think of you always."

And then he was gone, silently disappearing into the dark, cold rain.

Love never takes, it sacrifices—love only gives, my mother used to say. That's all I could think about as I watched Edmund fade in the night. I knew he was going to make the biggest sacrifice of them all. He was going to give his life to save mine. And there was nothing I could do to stop him.

8

A NEW CHANCE

"WHAT HAVE YOU DONE?" I WOKE TO FINN, CUTTING THE rope from my wrist.

It was a moment before my eyes adjusted to the orange hues of the morning and another moment before my mind recalled everything that had happened in the night.

"How could you?" he asked again. I couldn't tell if he was expecting an actual response, but he continued at a shout before I could speak. "Men, search the perimeter. We must find him before he escapes to the coast."

"Leave him," I pleaded. "Let him be. He has punished himself enough."

His piercing emerald eyes glared at me with such intensity that I shrank back.

"You chose to aid the very side that has brought you nothing but pain? It is in your blood to stand against them. And you yield? Whose side are you on?"

"I'm not sure anymore," I said. "You say you fight for all that is good, but in truth all you fight for is vengeance."

"You did not watch as your own mother and brother were murdered before your eyes!"

"But I watched as yours were…And I loved them too, Finn. A piece of me died with them that night, you know that. I want to see their death avenged, just as you, but not this way. Those responsible will pay for what they have done. God will make sure of it."

"How can you say those things after you set Edmund free?"

"I told you, he's not one of them," I said through clenched teeth. I stumbled a few steps away from the tree, away from Finn, trying to avoid any more argument. Then he said three words that stopped me dead in my tracks.

"You love him." His voice was tight, a rigid sound that cut through the deceptively peaceful forest. The muscles in his forearms tightened as his fingers formed fists by his sides.

"I feel for him," I said. "He is not the man we thought him to be. He is much more."

"After everything, you turn to him?" His voice grew cold in the question.

"He is sacrificing himself to save this world...to save me," I said. "He is on our side. We have to help him. We have to save him!"

"Why should I save him? He did not offer such courtesy to my family—or my people. Let him die."

"The murders were not his doing. He loved the royal family."

"Ha! Since when does love destroy a family— since when does it bring down a kingdom? You watched, just as I, the downfall. You witnessed him gain everything from it."

"What you consider to be his gain was his curse. Please. I'm asking you to trust me. Forget your hatred of him, if only for a moment, and take me to Mount Zyon."

"How can I trust you now?"

This was the very question I had asked Edmund. It felt strange to have it directed at me. As if I had become the enemy. Could I be trusted? Had a part of me given in to something I shouldn't have? Was Edmund my temptation as I was his? No, I was strong and focused. The question asked of me was asked out of confusion. It was just ironic, nothing more.

"You know you can trust me. We fight for the same cause. We always have."

"Do we? What did he do to you, Clara? What could he possibly say to you to make you believe that there is any good left in him?"

"He has given me information that will help us bring down the fallen."

"What do you know of the fallen and the situation here in this world? You have been living in a peaceful world while we fight and shed blood to keep what is left of this one alive."

"The war hasn't even begun, Finn. That is what I know," I snapped. "Erik is alive. He didn't die in Hades. He plans to absorb the powers of the great guardians. He will absorb Edmund's the first chance he gets. Can you imagine what he will do with that power? He will use it to come after me."

"Only the descendants of Lucifer have that ability. And you killed Victor, the last decedent. When Edmund dies, his powers die with him."

"Victor had a son."

Finn's expression darkened.

"That's impossible."

"I wish it were," I said looking into his eyes. "Victor's blood runs through Erik's veins. He is the last decedent. That is why he was sent to Coushatta. His true identity was being protected from the guardians, just as I was being protected from the fallen."

"How is this possible?"

"Erik's mother was the last female guardian."

Finn stumbled backward a few steps while looking off into the distance.

"How could we have missed this?" he mumbled to himself. "I should have known. I felt his strength in Hades—I saw the hatred in his eyes. I should have killed him when I had the chance."

"Find a new chance. Take me to Zy."

I saw his eyes wander the perimeter of the camp, eyeing the soldiers that looked for Edmund's tracks.

Finally, he squared his shoulders. "Men, gather your things," he barked. "We leave immediately."

There was a little resistance among the guard, questioning if they should stay to track Edmund, but Finn insisted that he knew where we could find him. And of course, thanks to me, he did know. Everyone loaded their packs with fresh water and their weapons and were ready to go before the morning dew had left the ground.

I had found a new way to Zy.

9

SHADOW WALKERS

WE TRUDGED THROUGH THE WOODS, CLEARING A PATH through vines and various wild plants. The trees on this side of the island, the north side, grew taller and thicker than the side we'd explored the day before. Most of the trees were redwood and maple—it was just as beautiful as the forest of pine light, only in its own unique way.

We stopped occasionally to rest. A part of me felt that we wouldn't have stopped as frequently if Kalani and I hadn't been a part of the excursion. Nevertheless, many of the men took this time to re-lieve themselves or to gather wild cloudberries to quiet the grumble in their stomachs. Finn made sure I ate every time we stopped. He was so paranoid that I might be hungry. *Heaven forbid I get hungry*, I thought. But I went along with it and ate my fair share of the fruit. Cloudberries reminded me of the time I spent in the woods as a child. And I thought about the sweet pastries my mother made with them. *Mother.* I hated that I had to leave her back in Ire-land. But I quickly reminded myself that it was for the best. To keep her safe.

Sometime in the afternoon we stopped near a shallow stream. I went down with a canteen, filling it with cold, clear water. Kalani followed me, doing the same. We didn't talk much, only the occasional word or two. I was still frustrated that she hadn't tried to help Edmund.

I knelt down, splashing my face to refresh myself as much as possible. Just as I lifted my eyes from the water, I noticed a strange fog roll through the forest, spreading in width from the distance and working its way forward to us. It grew thick within minutes, bringing the smell of rotten tomatoes with it.

"Shadow walkers!" Finn shouted. "Men, start a fire—ready your weapons."

He came running to us, covering the many yards between us in a matter of seconds.

"Come on," he said.

I shared a worried look with Kalani as we obediently followed him back to where his men had gathered. The sudden excitement and worry was already making me uneasy.

"What's going on?"

"It seems that Erik has sent shadow walkers to retrieve you and Kalani. They are near."

"Shadow walkers?"

"They are the ones who have no ties to country, no morals or emotions. They fight for the thrill of the kill. They are servants of the dark, much like the fallen."

"Father spoke of shadow walkers when I was young. I thought they were myth, only a story to scare children. You're telling me they exist?"

"Our country had been safe from them for centuries before the rise of darkness."

He grabbed my arm and Kalani's and led us to the newly made fire, where a barricade of packs and satchels had been strategically stacked in a moon shape around its flame. He then quickly grabbed the silver hilt of his sword, pulling it from the scabbard at his side, and covered the blade in oil. Men from around the camp did the same.

"Stay by the fire," he said, swinging the blade through its blue flames. I felt the heat of the sword blow past me as he steadied the flaming blade in front of us. "Fire is the element of their destruction. You will be safe here, I'll see to that." He anxiously paced the ground in front of the barricade, studying the layout of the land around us. "How are you with a bow and arrow?" he asked over his shoulder.

"It's been a while, but I can manage."

"Good. If any come near, shoot them with a flaming arrow, but don't leave the fire."

I nodded as I gathered two sets of bows and arrows from the ground.

Just as I handed a bow to Kalani, Finn was approached by a soldier.

"We spotted two, just outside the perimeter," the man said. "Do you want us to make the initial attack?"

"No, that's what they expect," Finn said. "Hold the perimeter around the grounds. We will let them come to us. Let's draw them out of the fog."

He shuffled around, rallying the men into position.

"Finn!" I shouted over the clank of weapons and low rumble of uneasy voices.

"Yes?" He turned my way for a moment.

"Be careful."

With a nod, he disappeared among his men.

Dark forms emerged from the black soil of the earth, like zombies rising from transient graves. They were hideous, corpselike predators of the night, moving with the shadows of the forest. Their bodies were sturdy and enormous in size; their skin was dark and flaky like dry earth. Long stringy hair framed their hollow faces, and pointed teeth glinted behind evil smiles. But none of this was as frightening as their eyes—their blood red eyes. Hell itself couldn't have released more frightful demons.

Kalani said a few words under her breath. I didn't understand them, but I could imagine what she meant. She drew closer to the barrier of satchels, crouching down with the arch of the bow by her side. She felt the same fear that twisted in my stomach.

Dozens of creatures advanced all around us, swarming the forest like flies in the night. They brought a terrible smell with them, like rotten food. I tried to refrain from breathing through my nose, but breathing through my mouth seemed twice as bad, like I could taste the bad smell.

The first shadow creature attacked, throwing a dark spear through the metal armor of a soldier. A loud yell broke through the night, a painful sound to all of our ears. It had begun.

"Attack!" Finn shouted.

We watched helplessly as his men charged the dark enemy with blazing swords held straight ahead. Finn was nothing short of a hero in the night, slashing steel into countless shadow walkers. As more heads erupted from the earth, he slid to his knees, beheading them before they could do any damage.

The ground buckled near us.

I grasped the bow tightly in my left hand while I held an arrow to the roaring fire. In seconds it was ablaze and ready to be launched. The wooden shaft of the arrow fit smoothly between my fingers. I notched the arrow and curled my fingers around the bowstring. I was ready to strike.

To our right, twenty paces past the fire behind us, a creature knocked a soldier from his feet. The creature raised his long black spear high above his head and paused as if he were taking pleasure from the moment. Before the spear spiraled down for its lethal blow, I aimed and released the blazing arrow into the air. It whistled as it flew steady and straight, then sunk deep into the chest of the shadow walker. The black shape instantly turned to ash, showering down on the soldier below it.

I quickly ran another arrow through the fire behind us, slid it to the bowstring, and prepared myself for another opportunity. I was prepared to take out as many hellish monsters as I possibly could.

To my left, Kalani readied her bow for the same cause.

One by one, the dark bodies crawled from the ground around us. As they approached, we took aim and shot them in the same order of their resurrection. Kalani and I had abolished a number of the demons before something hard hit the side of my head.

The scene swam before my eyes. My legs crumbled beneath me, and my body collapsed to the ground. *What's happening to me?* Everything turned upside down in an instant. The loud clash of steel muffled, the crackle of the fire vanished, and the bow in my hand dropped to the ground. The fire seemed as one big blur as my body was lifted high in the air and thrown over a rotting shoulder. I instinctively coughed as I unwillingly breathed in the heavy, rotten stench of a shadow walker. *This is it. They've gotten me.* My eyes burned from the smell. I wanted to close them, to give in to the dizzy feeling in my head, but I fought to keep them open.

The predators carried me through ash-filled air, fighting off soldiers as we headed past the creek. I saw Finn in the distance, charging after us, cutting limbs from dozens of creatures as he neared. He was as fast as a jaguar and brave as a king.

Then he was upon us, angry and fearless. His blade of fire slashed through the neck of the creature that carried me. Once I dropped to the ground, I crawled a few yards away, and then collapsed into a patch of tall wildflowers. I watched through blurry tunnels as Finn's blade met with the dark weapon of the second creature, bringing sparks of fire to the air like mad fireflies.

The creature was strong with his strange sword, but Finn was quick and skillful. I forced myself to keep my eyes open, watching two fuzzy figures switch from offense to defense, until the darkest of figures, the shadow walker, made a wrong move. The creature swung the tip of his weapon high over Finn's head, leaving his body exposed. That was all that Finn needed. He ducked the creature's weapon, slicing his blade through its black kneecaps. As the

124

shadow walker fell to the ground, Finn took his last swing, severing the head of the shadow walker. The air filled with the dusty remains of the enemy.

"Are you alright?" he asked, quickly kneeling down to inspect me.

"Mmm," was the only sound I could muster.

His face came into focus long enough for me to see the concern in his eyes. His expression made me feel uncomfortable, nervous even. Did I look that bad? My stomach muscles tightened as I attempted to sit up—to prove that I was all right, but stars swarmed across my vision, and I sank back down to my former position.

"Easy, Clara."

He slid his sword back into its scabbard, and then swept the hair from my face. I felt an arm slide gently under my back and another under my knees. The next thing I knew, my head was resting on his shoulder.

"Keep your eyes open," I heard him say. But I had already closed them to stop my head from spinning. I drifted to the sound of rushing water.

10

WOUNDS

"OPEN YOUR EYES," ECHOED IN MY EAR. IT WAS FINN'S VOICE, ever so gentle, but equally persistent. "Open your eyes, Clara."

When I blinked my eyes open, Finn was slipping his shirt over his head.

Though my vision was blurred, I admired the lines of his tan chest as he leaned down to dip his shirt into the stream. I thought back to when I first saw him like this—the jungle. That image of him leading me through the muggy island, of letting me fall asleep in his arms, the image of his face disappearing as I drifted to my near death, every unblemished detail still perfectly preserved in my memory, and now I had one more.

"That's it—keep them open," he said. "Stay awake."

He touched the damp shirt gently to my forehead, letting the water trickle down into my hair. The cool water felt good against my throbbing head.

I sighed a breath of bliss.

Finn pulled me close, cradling my head as if I were a fragile thing. His fingers stroked my hair while I lay still. The steady movement calmed my spirits, relaxing my body from head to toe. For a brief moment, I felt safe and secure—at peace.

But then my mind flew back to where we were and what had happened. *Shadow walkers. The fight. Kalani.* I tried to raise myself.

"Please lay still. You are safe now," Finn said, reading my mind.

"But the shadow walkers—"

"Everything is fine," he repeated. "They have re-treated beyond the forest. They won't come back tonight. And the wounded are already being looked after. Just lay still—your head is still bleeding."

"And Kalani?"

"You needn't worry about her. She's getting plenty of attention from the men." A low chuckle rumbled from his throat.

He dipped his shirt into the stream again and placed it to my neck.

"Does anything else hurt?"

"Just my head."

I reached up, feeling for the source of the pain and quickly discovered the lump on the right side of my head, just above my hairline. It felt warm and sticky. I brought my hand back down to see the bright blood covering my fingers. They had hit me really hard, with a club I imagined. I could expect a headache in the morning, I was sure of it.

I searched his face, the sharp arch of his lips, the straight line of his nose—his eyes. He placed a small canteen to my lips.

"Drink," he insisted. "I'm afraid you're dehy-drated. You need to keep your strength about you. You will need it for the trip we have ahead of us."

He helped me prop my body to one side so that the water dripped right into my mouth. The cool water tasted sweet when it crossed my lips, as if he had squeezed a few of the cloudberries into it. Just the way I liked it. Had he remembered, or was it a lucky guess?

I looked up from under my lashes to steal another glimpse of his perfect face. Being that close to Finn was just as wonderful as it had been a year ago. There was tension and an electric force between us—something I couldn't deny or ignore. I only hoped my flushed skin wouldn't decide to blush while he looked down at me. There was an unquestionable roughness to him, a roughness that can only be acquired from life itself, but this hard shell made him even more desirable.

His hand strayed down my neck, without the cool towel this time. The touch of his hand to my skin made my fingers tremble beside me. *I hope he doesn't notice.*

Neither one of us said anything for several minutes, but I saw him secretly glance at me out of the corner of my eye. *What's he thinking right now? Should I say something?*

"Thanks for saving me, back there," I finally said, breaking the silence. "I owe you, again."

"You owe me nothing."

There was an awkward silence as he looked to the stream. Now that he knew I was going to be okay, he seemed indifferent again. How could I make him understand that what he saw and what he thought he knew was completely wrong? I had done nothing, so why did his silence make me feel like the guilty one? Like I needed to apologize.

"It's not what you think, you know. With Edmund and me, I mean." I stumbled over the words before opting to give an apology. "Is it too late to say I'm sorry?"

"I don't think you understand the complication you've caused. An apology simply won't do."

"Then what?" I cried, pulling my head away from him. *Too fast.* My head started to swim again, so I lowered it again to clarify the question. "What is it that you want?"

"That should be quite obvious."

Silence again.

I hadn't expected that response. I hadn't prepared to go down that road—a road with no known end—so I kept the subject focused on his accusation.

"What complications have I caused, anyway? I've done nothing wrong."

"You have fraternized with the enemy," he said. "The Senate will call it treason."

"He isn't the enemy, Finn. That's what I've been trying to tell you."

"Enough with that!" he said, gritting his teeth. "I cannot help you if you continue to speak that way."

"It's the truth!" I snapped. "Who says I need your help anyhow?"

"You will. Once the Senate discovers you were working with Edmund, you will be hunted, found, and placed on trial. They will not offer the same forgiveness as I do."

"Since when do we live in a country that prosecutes the innocent? Is that what you are fighting for?"

"No, I'm fighting to save you, but you are making it a hard fight to win."

He was provoking me, yet again. I watched his face contort to an expression of frustration. *Good, we're both frustrated.* Knowing that I wasn't the only one somehow made me feel better.

"No one can save me," I said. "I know of the prophecy, Finn. You can't keep me safe."

He looked bewildered that I had brought up the subject.

"It is only myth."

"I saw it with my own eyes, so don't try to convince me it's not real."

"He took you to the garden?"

"Yes, and I'm glad he did. He allowed me to see what I'm up against instead of hiding it from me. I'm so tired of being left in the dark."

"He should never have taken you there."

"Would you rather my death come as a surprise? Because I know that I wouldn't, and since we are talking about *my* life here, I don't really care what you think he should or shouldn't have done. He was trying to help me."

"He is not trying to help you. He's our enemy, Clara. All he has to offer you are his lies and illusions. He will only show you what he wants you to see— tell you what he wants you to hear. You of all people should know this!"

"You're wrong!"

I wanted to slap him. Hit him. Something. The compulsion grew by the second, but I fought it, grabbing at the ground below me. I was angered by his words—his loss of feeling and his inability to listen to reason. I understood hate—I hated everyone who had harmed my family. I had hated Edmund. But now, now that I knew who he really was, I couldn't hate him anymore, not in the least.

"He wants to save me, just as much as you. Maybe more. After all, he wasn't the one who left me."

I could see that I had struck a nerve.

"He lusts for you!"

My hand struck his face faster than my brain could comprehend. If it weren't for the tingle in my fingertips, I wouldn't have believed that I had been the one to strike him. A light pink handprint appeared on the right side of his face. I didn't feel guilty though. No, he deserved it. He was the one to make false accusations. He was the one to make inappropriate suggestions and to belittle me in every way a man could belittle a woman. Yes, he deserved it all right.

I crawled out of his arms, which had loosened around me from my surprise strike, and then staggered away from him.

I tried my best to subdue the anger building, but it was a hard thing to do, knowing that he felt that way about Edmund and about me. *How dare he say those things.*

I couldn't figure Finn out. One minute he was snapping at me, the next he was implying that he wanted me. Wanted me for what? He had already trampled over my heart, causing me infinite pain when he left me in Ireland. I loved him—hadn't he known? Surely. Even though the time we had before was limited, it was enough time to see that. I had put my heart on the line, and all he did was push it away. His sorry excuse for protecting me, then and now—left a bad taste in my mouth. It seemed everyone wanted to protect me from pain, but in doing so they brought on the worst kind of pain. The incurable kind. And I don't care what anyone says, time does not heal all wounds. Not this kind of wound. Not this kind of hurt. Not this kind of pain. Screw him. Enough with these ridiculous thoughts of love. *Who needs them?* Maybe this was my cure.

I buried my face in my hands as soon as I reached my tent, which I found slung neatly over a low tree branch, waiting for me. I wanted to cry, but my face was still burning from my fury. There were too many things bothering me. Too many questions. And I had a future that was utterly depressing. Maybe Finn was right. Maybe I shouldn't have seen the prophecy. Maybe things would be a lot easier—a lot simpler if I didn't know that at the end of it all I was going to die. *Maybe I was too harsh,* I thought.

I was glad when sleep overpowered me. I dreamed myself away from the mess that I was in, until my mind was silent.

Morning came too soon, peeping through the small holes in the fabric of the tent. I didn't feel rested enough for the new day. As predicted, my head still pounded with pain from the attack.

I could hear movement outside my tent. Soldiers bickering over the remainder of rum, the dull clanging of a sword against someone's pant leg, the sound of a spoon raking the bottom of bowl, and if I listened hard enough, the steady flow of the stream.

After stretching, I stepped into the morning light.

The dull light streaked through the proud standing redwoods all around the camp while a soft wind scattered grey dust from the remains of our enemies across the grass. The land in the forest was speckled with the holes and crevices left by the shadow walkers who'd risen, probably fifty or so in all—a scary reminder of what had taken place over the night.

And there was Finn, slumped over, asleep against the tree nearest my tent. I wanted to be mad at him. I wanted to maintain that same fury I'd felt the night before. But I couldn't. He looked so help-less as he slept, his arms crossed tightly across his chest, his sword out by his side. All of that anger had been replaced with remorse for my actions.

The sound of movement from behind startled me. It was a soldier, a very tall, butch guy, with rust-colored hair. I had noticed him before, but this was the first time he had approached me. Gabriel was his name, but I heard most of the men call him Red. I assumed this nickname stemmed from his bright col-ored hair.

"He stayed watch all night," Red said. "Let's let the lad sleep a bit longer."

"All night?"

He nodded. "It's not my place to meddle, but he cares something great for you, Lady Clara."

I looked down at my feet, ashamed that I could have ever hurt him. Red must have noticed my shame because he pulled me in for a bear hug. I was startled but warmed by the gesture.

Red released me. "How 'bouts we get some food for you? Hmm? I believe the men caught some squirrels earlier. Let's have a taste!"

"That sounds nice."

"I can introduce you to some of the others while we're at it."

I sat by the fire, watching Finn sleep from a distance as the smell of roasted meat filled my nose. It actually smelled really good. My stomach grumbled. Kalani found her way over to me and made herself comfortable against an abandoned satchel lying on the ground. We exchanged a few quick smiles, but no words. I was happy to see she was still all in one piece.

Red wiggled his way in between us, pulling us both under each arm for a quick squeeze, and then started pointing fingers and naming names. I guess now that we had somewhat fought together against the shadow walkers, we had become a part of the team—we had passed initiation with him. It took him a good ten minutes to point out everyone around the fire, and milling about the camp. The whole time my mind was wrapped around thoughts of Finn. I hoped Red wouldn't quiz us later.

We ate handfuls of the flavorful meat while the men around us told hunting stories and strange jokes that neither Kalani nor I seemed to understand. I had already eaten my share of breakfast and was licking my fingers clean when Finn joined us.

"Must have been some dream you had, sire. Or did you get into the rum last night?" Red said jokingly. Everyone chuckled with him.

"Ha, ha," Finn replied sarcastically.

"Best sit down and grab some meat before the ladies finish it off." Another joke. This time Red winked at me while he laughed.

Finn punched the burly Red playfully as he reached for his breakfast. I excused myself from the group, leaving before he had taken his first bite.

I glanced over my shoulder a few times as I walked away and noticed that Kalani had moved closer to Finn. Strangely, for the first time, I wondered what she thought about him. Did they have a connection? Did she feel that strange pull to him, as I did? I hadn't been paying attention. I guess there was no way of really knowing unless I asked. And that wasn't going to happen.

There was a sharp pain of jealousy in my stomach. Kalani was so beautiful. Everything about her was perfect: the way she held her head high, her stride, her glossy golden skin, her hair that never seemed out of place—she looked like the princess she was, and she was a gorgeous one at that. Finn deserved someone like her. I felt so plain when I looked at Kalani, so hollow and unimportant. I knew that I felt this way because I was. I was just the pale, lonely moon next to her radiant sunlight. What was I thinking? I could never compete with her. I'd never been in the running, really. Her marriage with Finn was practically decided already anyway. A guardian could never marry a king. Ugh!

My canteen was sitting just outside my tent; I grabbed that and headed for the stream to fill it up. *Keep yourself busy*, I thought. That was what I needed to do. No one needed to know that I was still upset. Especially Finn. *Just keep yourself busy.*

11

DEAL

THE MORNING PLODDED ONWARD UNTIL THE MEN DISPERSED from around the fire. I kept my distance, gathering and filling their canteens by the stream. Camp was packed quickly and efficiently, and within the hour we were moving through the forest. Not a single trace of our existence was left behind.

The trees and brush grew thicker now that we had left the area around the stream, and with the increased vegetation came more insects. Mosquitoes swarmed by the hundreds, sweat dripped into my eyes, and a terrible ache was beginning to splinter down my calves, so I was unutterably thankful when we finally reached the ocean. It had almost been a full day.

A ship glided toward us through the twilight, sailing straight for the embankment. A ship I knew well. The angel-shaped prow cut through the rich blue waves with ease, spraying beads of water back against its dark cherry hull. The setting sun kissed its masts, casting shadows on its grand sails. It was apparent that it was as royal and as fearless as its master and commander. Four longboats floated respectfully next to their great mother ship, moving steadily to the shore.

At the head of our party, Finn swam out to greet the boats, treading water as the closest longboat filled with cheerful sailors reached him. He climbed in and pointed the rowers onward. Three others followed behind, ready to pick up passengers. I was instructed to board the first boat, along with Kalani and Red. The four sailors already on the longboat wasted no time in getting us to the royal ship.

Nearly fifty men rushed to the side of the ship as our longboat was pulled up from the sea. A robust man with a very kind smile helped me from the rocking boat onto deck. Dodger, I think he said was his name.

"Welcome, Lady Clara," he said. And a buzz of excitement rang through the crowd of sailors. Kalani was helped next, met with equal enthusiasm, followed by Red. One by one the other soldiers and longboats were hoisted aboard, every man welcomed with a pat on the back or a swig of rum. Finn, who was last to come aboard, was surrounded as soon as his boots reunited with the spotless deck planks of his ship.

Kalani and I were handed silver cups filled with warm apple cider and were offered biscuits and other small treats, a sign of the men's excitement for our arrival. As I sipped the spicy cider, I watched Finn talk with his men, filling them in on the happenings of our journey. It was clear from the way the men responded that they all had a deep love and devotion to their ship's commander and to their country's rightful king. There was no doubt in my mind that he possessed the makings of a great leader. He was admired just as his father had been.

"We sail for Zy tonight," he announced to his crew.

"Zy, sire?" a sailor asked.

"Yes. We shall attack with everything we have."

A murmur of unhappy surprise ran through the assembled men. The man named Dodger nudged his way forward and quietly pulled Finn away from the crowd of sailors. "What be the reason to attack such a dark place, cap'n?" he asked, his eyes wide with shock. "We aren't familiar with that land…and with no map, our enemy already be at an advantage."

"We have information that Victor's blood runs through another—a dark prince. He's been hiding at Mount Zyon all this time, forming an army that is like no other." Finn paused while the sturdy man processed the news. "We have all grown up hearing stories of the prophecy, and I fear that those stories are true. The time is near, Dodger—we must strike before his army reaches the shores of Everest. It is our best chance."

"What be your plan, sire?"

Finn's eyes darted across the ship to where Kalani stood unconsciously poised and beautiful.

"Princess Kalani wishes to guide us through the terrain. She will lead us to the castle gates. A few men will stay behind to guard Lady Clara and the ship while the remainder will follow me into battle. We will rain down on this army before they see the storm clouds. This time, we will be the ones with the advantage, not them."

Did I just hear him right? He expected me to stay behind on the ship? If it weren't for me, we wouldn't even be here. He wouldn't know about

Erik or his army. I shoved my way through two sail-ors that had been casually talking about the crew's new heading. My feet stomped to a halt when I reached Finn, my hands naturally positioned them-selves on my hips.

"If you think I'm going to stand on the sidelines, you're greatly mistaken," I said breaking the stagnant noise of the chatty crew.

"Clara—tomorrow you *will* stay aboard the ship. That is an order. I will not negotiate with you on this. My two best men will stay behind to guard you."

"That's ridiculous. You're out of your mind if you think I will obey such a command. Besides, you need me out there. I'm twice as good as your best man—you know I am."

"You are a good fighter, Clara, but you're not going."

"Yes—I am."

"Do you not remember the attack last night?" He reached out and touched the sore spot hidden slightly behind my hairline. I winced when it throbbed from his gentle touch. "The wound on your head has yet to heal. I will not risk your safety."

I drew my sword. "Fight me then. We will see who needs protecting."

Suddenly the deck was filled with surprised whispers from the crew as the men drew closer to hear our conversation. Finn noticed, and he tried to downplay his own surprise to my proposal.

"I'm not going to fight you," he said, chuckling to himself. The crew around us mimicked his reac-tion.

I raised my sword, sliding it against the stubble on his cheek, working my way down to his neck.

"If you beat me, I will stay aboard your precious ship," I said. "But only if you beat me."

Finn knew that he'd have to throw me in the brig to keep me on his ship, but he also knew that if he won, I would honor the agreement.

He studied my face for a second, before knocking my blade away with his armguard.

"Deal."

12

CHECKMATE

My heart raced with nerves as I stood facing Finn, but, my mind was calm—I focused on what needed to be done in order to defeat him at this game.

We first began by playfully tapping the ends of our blades together, testing to see who would make the first move. With Finn being a gentleman, I knew he would wait for me to make the first strike.

I twirled the steel of his blade around, knocking it away from mine. He countered. His moves were predictable when we first began to fight. They were moves I knew well, but I was taught how those same moves could be slightly modified to make an extreme difference in offense and defense. My father had taught me to use my quirky habit of counting and my oddly observant behavior against my opponent. He said that how I saw the world gave me an edge on anyone in a fight. It took me a long time to understand what he meant by that.

I carefully noted the ten steps between my feet and Finn's. I counted fifteen steps from where I stood to a barrel that held three broken arrows on its lid. *Those might be useful,* I thought.

The crowd of sailors grew with each second as the entire ship caught on to what we were doing. The rails of the ship lined with curious observers while some climbed the ratlines to get a better view.

As the fight intensified, sailors from below the ship were rushed to the deck to catch the duel. Everyone was interested in viewing the show.

And a show was what we gave them.

I lunged forward, careful to provoke a counter-attack that would put me closer to the broken arrows on the barrel to his right. Finn's blade met with mine, forcing me into the barrel, just as I'd hoped. My left hand flew behind me and tucked an arrow into my left sleeve without missing a single beat of his blade. No one noticed my new weapon.

I began to strike with more speed in an effort to wear him down. I wanted to get my blade ahead of his so that he would be in a constant state of defense, but he kept up with my growing speed.

We fenced our way past the helm and up the decorative steps to the bow of the ship, clashing the steel of our blades as we darted around barrels and riggings. We lunged back and forth, like cat and mouse around the bow, before fighting our way back down to the crowd on the main deck. We didn't stop for anything. It was one big game to us; it could have easily been chess or checkers. At least, that's how we were going about it. All strategy.

He managed to beat me back against the door of the captain's cabin. From the crowd's reaction, I could tell they thought he was disarming me. The sailors raised a chant, encouraging Finn to make the move that would finish the game. But I had already prepared for this. Just when everyone, including Finn, thought I was completely helpless, I hit the flat end of my hilt hard against his blade, momentarily redirecting the end of his sword down, and then

142

lunged forward, flipping my hidden weapon from my sleeve and pressing the tip of the broken arrow against his throat.

"Check mate."

The ship roared with enthusiasm and laughter at my victory.

I had won my right to fight.

Finn smiled at me flirtatiously, conceding defeat. I stood still with my arrow pressed to his neck, breathing hard, a dozen butterflies fluttering in my stomach now that my body's fighting mode had switched off. I blushed and swiftly backed away, lowering my weapon in the hopes that my stomach would settle back to normal.

"A deal is a deal, but know that I am not happy about this."

"I never asked you to be happy," I responded. "I only asked to fight."

I found myself grinning like a schoolgirl at him before our stare was broken by Red, scooping me up and lifting me to his block-like shoulders.

"You're a real guardian, Lady Clara. A real guardian," he said, parading me around the group of sailors.

There was a lot of song and sailor jokes in the remainder of the hour, followed by dancing and drinking games. Finn left almost immediately after the celebrating began, grabbing a map before disappearing below deck. I noticed Dodger, Kalani, and two other soldiers follow. Apparently I wasn't invited. This was another slap in the face.

Even though so many jovial people surrounded me, I was still completely separated from everyone.

I'd won over a few friends; at least Red and Dodger took to me kindly. And there was a handful of sailors who were polite to me, but the guard was already hard at work, turning them against me.

Even now, I could see them making their way around the deck, speaking to small groups of sailors at a time. I knew they were warning the men, telling them I was dangerous. A traitor, even. By the look in those sailors' eyes, they were pretty convincing. Too bad I couldn't win *them* over as easily as Red and Dodger.

As nightfall swept over the water, drawing the last of the day from us, the group slowly began to separate.

I snuck away from everyone into the familiarity of the captain's cabin, Finn's cabin. His scent was everywhere in the room, and something about that made it feel like I was home. The wood stain of the cabin was preserved better than the rest of the ship, which was inevitably bleaching in the saltwater and the sun. Everything was in the same place as it had been the last time I was here. The large wardrobe to my left, the bed to the right, the small windows lining the walls—everything was just as I'd remembered it.

I ran my hands over the smooth wood, soaking up the warm welcoming feeling it gave, before sitting at the foot of the bed. *Has it really been that long since I was here?* My hands rested on the soft ruby blanket of the bed. I wanted to wrap myself in its warmth; I wanted to bury my face in the feather pillow at the other end of the bed and drift into a dreamless sleep...

The door of the cabin flew open. Kalani stepped inside with her arm wrapped around Finn. She looked somewhat disappointed to see me, but Finn flashed me one of his heart-stopping grins.

I returned the smile as best I could, rising from the bed.

"I'm glad you're here," he said. "I wanted to see that the two of you were taken care of. I want you both to be comfortable. It's important that everyone gets their rest tonight."

"Of course," I said, clearing my throat. "I was just leaving...Is there space below where I can sleep?"

"Well, one of the men offered his hammock. But I had planned to make the cabin suitable for you both to share. I can hang a hammock or fashion another cot in here, if you'd like."

"Kalani can have the cabin. I don't mind sleeping below."

"The cabin has plenty of room and is much more suitable for a lady," he said. "Trust me, the men can get loud and—"

"Below will be fine."

"It can be difficult to sleep when—"

"It will be fine," I assured him.

He frowned. "If that is what you wish."

I walked past the two, feeling the weight of a heavy heart. It was jealously again that possessed me; I knew it was, but I couldn't shake it. Why couldn't I get it through my thick head that this was how it was supposed to be? *Finn belongs with Kalani. Not with me.*

I felt like I was walking the plank as I practically dragged myself down the length of the deck. Dodger greeted me halfway and led me down into the belly of the ship. I faintly remembered it from before, but it wasn't as familiar to me as the captain's quarters.

During our walk down the stairs, I learned that Dodger was the quartermaster and that he had a wife and little girl back in Everest. He said I kind of reminded him of his little Anna. I appreciated his small talk, since I couldn't bring myself to carry on a conversation at the moment.

"This be our quarters, Lady Clara. It's not much on the eyes, but you'll be surprised how well a hammock can rock you to sleep." He grinned. "Can I get you anything before I go?"

I took a moment to inspect the beige hammock that would serve as my bed for the night. A nice woolen blanket lay across the net. I picked it up and shook it loose. "Looks like I have everything I need. Thanks for your kindness, Dodger. Your daughter is lucky to have you."

His chapped lips turned upward one last time as he said goodnight and left me to rest.

The sailor's bunk was just that: a sailor's bunk. It reeked of manly smells—sweat, tobacco, and more rum to be precise—and it was close quarters. Rows of cots lined the hull of the ship, and hammocks hung and rocked above them. It was a tight fit, but thankfully the men moved around to accommodate me with the best hammock and wool blanket on board. A very nice gesture, considering many of them still didn't trust me.

I couldn't blame them for their suspicion. I probably wouldn't have trusted me either. After all, I had freed someone they considered to be their enemy, coincidently, the same person I had once considered to be mine. I had managed to bring a lot of controversy to Finn's men, especially since the guard informed them of my "treasonous ways," but somehow they still seemed to respect me for my guardian upbringing and for winning the joust against Finn. At least I had that. I'd deal with the guard and the Senate later.

The ship had a voice below, moaning and creaking with its movement through the dark waters. A group of men huddled in a circle, placing bets on a dice game. Their laughter filled the bunk every few minutes. It was a lot of noise, just like Finn had warned.

I rocked back and forth in the hammock, staring at the natural flaws in the wood of the ceiling, counting the barrels of rum in the bunker—there were twenty-three in plain sight—and then counting the fish nets hanging from the rafters. Fifteen. I was trying my best to keep my mind off of Finn, but when the laugher finally stopped and the moan of the ship lessened and all seemed quiet, my willpower caved. Finn was on my mind.

My jealous thoughts were suffocating. Bunking with such a large crew didn't help either. I felt like I was drowning. I needed to breathe, just like I needed to be near him. I wrapped the woolen blanket around my shoulders and stepped out on the cool deck for some air.

The sky met the ocean in what seemed like an endless flow of blue. I always loved being out in the middle of the ocean, especially at night when the water was calm and it seemed as though the heavy ship was flying, with nothing to stop it from reaching the stars. The stars shined bright tonight, reflecting on the gentle swells of the ocean. I stepped over to the side rail for a moment to take in the clean air. The coolness of it swept through me, relieving me of my former feelings of asphyxiation. I made my way to the quarterdeck, twirling around in the wind that swept under the masts and admiring the fancy knot work along the way. As I climbed the center stairway, I was met with a welcoming hand from the top deck.

"Finn." I hesitated a moment before placing my free hand in his.

"Couldn't sleep?"

"Needed air," was all I managed to say as his fingers cradled mine.

There was an awkward moment then; tension grew as we both stood and stared at each other. Suddenly, I couldn't remember how to speak, to breathe, or to move. I was trapped in my own body by the magic of his stare. The woolen blanket around me fell to the deck floor, but I stood still. My body had become a prison, keeping me from the one thing I wanted most—Finn. He had some nerve to place this curse upon me—to cage me in my own body. How dare he look at me this way! *Look away, look away from him now*, I chanted to myself. But I couldn't. He was so glorious in the night.

With each passing second, the expression in his eyes appeared to reflect more and more pain, like the same invisible force that imprisoned me had turned to attack him. His jaw tightened. His free arm flexed and pressed firmly against his side. Was he straining to speak or not to speak? To move or not to move?

The curse that we had unknowingly placed on each other lifted, and we both fell forward with an encouraging rock from the boat. Finn opened his arms, and I collapsed right into them. Everything about him felt safe and familiar to me. With his arms around me, we were one body, with our hearts beating in perfect rhythm. It had been so long since I'd been able to enjoy his closeness, to concentrate on every perfect feature without distraction—his smell, a spicy fragrance acquired from the earth and sea, the warmth of his olive skin, the hard muscles on his arms. They all were wrapped around me now.

His hair fell into his eyes, momentarily shadowing their fierce green color. I instinctively slid a hand to his face, moving the strand so that there was nothing dividing our gaze. A part of me wanted to continue the motion of my fingers through his dark hair, to pull his face close to mine, to touch my lips to his. I wanted to taste the trace of cinnamon I remembered so well, the taste I had dreamt about over the last year spent away from him. But this was not the time, nor the place. And I knew it should never be. He belonged to another. I just needed to keep my emotions at bay, concentrate on tomorrow—on finding my father, on saving what was left of this kingdom. Focus on the horrible fact that Finn and I could never be—this was as far as it could ever go.

But his desirable lips leaned in too close for me to hold that concentration—too close for me to resist. His eyes held mine a moment too long. *If he doesn't kiss me soon, it might be the death of me.* My heart would surely explode right inside my chest. I could feel it, pounding under my ribs harder, faster.

"Checkmate," his smooth lips whispered.

Then, right before my heart gave out, his lips met mine, sending my mind spiraling into a place of pure bliss. I felt like I was soaring high above us, looking down at a perfect moment in my life. A thrilling, unspoken passion erupted between us, burning my lips as they clung to his for dear life. His arms looped around my waist, pulling me even closer to this passion, pushing our lips even harder together. His warm lips still held that magical taste of cinnamon. It was better than I remembered, which seemed impossible.

Our heads tilted naturally in response to the movement of our lips, as they continued to explore. My ears burned when one hand moved from my waist to slide through my hair. He held me to him as if he knew I needed it, as if he knew I needed him to live. I had hoped that had been my own secret, but now, I was glad the secret was ours to share.

My mind blanked out all worries of this forbidden desire, only intensifying the sensitivity of my skin to his. A light stroke of his hand to my cheek felt so powerful, like I had never been touched before. The electric tingle trailed on my face each time he lifted his hand. This had to be something more than just want or desire. The way my skin felt when he grazed it with his—that feeling of closeness, that was all I ever wanted. And every piece of me knew that. Could he feel this invigorating, otherworldly force we created when we came together? No magic or drug could possibly simulate that sense. All of this had to mean something greater than I could process right now. Why would we be drawn together in such a way if we were not meant to stay together? How could this passion be denied? His touch filled every void in me, completing me, perfecting me.

This was it, the only moment I was allowed to be complete, to feel whole. My knees began to weaken; I was caving. I had to push him away before I lost my strength. I had to do it now, or I would never be able to let him go.

I pulled back slowly, collecting that moment around me to tuck away for always, for safekeeping. I suddenly realized that something should be said after a kiss like that, but I had no words.

His eyes were like emeralds, glowing in the night. His arms remained open in invitation. I staggered three more steps back, knowing that the one step was not enough between us.

Finally words tumbled from my mouth, but they didn't feel like they were the right ones.

"You shouldn't have done that," I said.

"Then you shouldn't look so beautiful," he said.

My cheeks burned from his compliment. I could only hope that my natural blush didn't show in the moonlight.

"You've imprisoned me with that kiss," he whispered.

I couldn't believe these words were for me, but that was what made them so great. His look was hypnotic, his scent enchanting, I had no guard against any of it—against him.

He slowly lessened the space between us, watching my reaction as he neared. I imagined he was checking to see if before had only been an accident. I'm sure my face read like an open book, saying that I had wanted every bit of what happened. He lightly kissed my cheek as his arm looped around my waist once more. Without a word he guided me past the dark mast to the bow of the ship. The wind in the night was strongest at this point, whipping around us like a magical force that wanted us close together. There was a chill to it, but Finn shielded me from it with the warmth of his body pressed against mine.

My eyes were now skimming the water, watching the swells burst as the ship drove through them. What was he thinking right now? I wished I were brave enough to ask.

It felt good to be in his arms again, all fighting, all farce, all pretense gone, no more denying our connection to each other. But this was all I could ever have. Deep down I knew that this was it for us. This night was the only thing that would ever be ours. So I was going to take in every moment of it. No regrets tonight.

I tilted my head up, inviting him to kiss me once more. His lips didn't hesitate, meeting mine with deliberate hunger. It was blissful and uncontrollable for a moment, before slowing to its end. Finn's lips broke from mine, but his gaze remained.

"To have you in my arms, the way you are now…" he whispered. "You are the only one I ever wish to hold."

"Will that always be your wish?"

"Until the world stops turning, and then after. This will always be my wish."

He was giving me everything by holding me, by confessing that this was what he wanted—that I was what he wanted. It was what I had waited for all this time. The pain I had experienced from losing him before had not been in vain. It all led up to this moment, to these words. The stars shined even brighter for us now; the ocean sparkled like a sea of diamonds. His confession was verbal, but the world around us made it feel visual.

Soon our bodies buckled to rest on the wooden floor of the quarterdeck. I remained in his arms, listening to the sound of the ocean while his hands played with mine. The curved bow held us together as the steady rock of the ship pushed me into drowsiness. My eyes strained to stay open. I wanted this night to last forever—to be an eternal night that looped and looped until the end of time. But sleep overtook me, just as he slipped away.

I dreamt of Finn that night. I dreamt that after this was all over, we would be together. But even in my dream I knew that it could never happen. I knew that it was forbidden. A king could never marry a guardian; the Senate would never allow it. Especially when his planned union would unite kingdoms—an entire world. All I could ever do was dream.

13

ZY

Sometime in the early hours of the morning, I was startled awake.

"Get dressed, er, freshen up, er, whatever it is you ladies do," the voice said. It took me a moment to wake up and recognize that it was Red. My eyes scanned the quarterdeck, yearning for Finn, but Red's face was all that I found. Finn must have slipped away after I'd fallen asleep. He knew just as I the dangers of being seen together. Especially since I was deemed a traitor now, and he was practically engaged to Kalani. Maybe I should feel relieved that I hadn't woken next to him. That would have really stirred things up with the guard. Maybe I should be glad the dream ended when it did. At least I was left with a perfect memory to hold on to forever.

"We made great speed through the night," Red said. "Zy is already on the horizon. Better grab some grub below. Cap'n will drop anchor soon."

I couldn't help but feel that I had just closed my eyes, and now it was already a brand new day. My time with Finn had been merely a fleeting second in my life—it was gone, the memory already foggy, like the blurred images left over after a dream. But it had been real, just like the day ahead of us.

In the captain's cabin, Kalani had already gotten dressed, wearing the same clothes she had worn on our first meeting. The wardrobe contained an array of clean shirts and pants, but none of them seemed to interest her. Wearing men's clothes didn't bother me, especially when it meant I could get out of the tattered dress I had been wearing for days. I quickly slipped into a tan top and brown pants and cinched them around my waist with my belt so that I could still carry my sword, and then made my way out the door. Kalani followed me down into the hull of the ship.

As we descended the stairs, the strong aroma of rum and spice greeted us. The galley was a small area, located just before the sleeping quarters, with lots of long benches and overhead cabinets for the pickled food and dry goods. We passed several men shoveling cheese and bread into their mouths before Dodger stepped in front of us.

"G'mornin'," he said politely.

"Good morning."

"Our cook be down with the scurvy, leavin' poor Caesar, here, as his stand-in." Dodger's huge hands playfully shook the shoulders of a short boy standing to the side of us. From the look of the food-stained, half-singed apron around the boy's waist, it was safe to assume he'd been having trouble in the galley. "This lad can't fix food to save his life."

"That's a bit harsh," the boy replied.

"At least you try," Dodger reassured him, chuckling. "Go take a rest, lad. I'll be takin' care of the ladies."

"Thank you, Quartermaster." Caesar handed Dodger his apron and flew from the galley.

"Alright, now that he's gone, what can I be gettin' for ya, loves?"

Kalani remained quiet, staring blankly at the men around us, who were clearly not used to eating around a princess. Since she'd decided to be silent, I chose to speak for the both of us.

"What's on the menu?"

"Well, we be havin' plenty of ripe melons, apples, and bananas. Cheese, bread, and some nicely seasoned jerk meat. I could rustle up a nice stew for ya. And if we be real lucky, I might could round ya up a bit of ham. If the lads haven't found me stash, that is."

"We eat?" Kalani asked. I figured there was no use trying to figure out what she would prefer. At this point, neither one of us should really be picky.

"Any of that would be fine."

He came back with a bowl of assorted fruits and two plates, one holding ham and cheese and the other seasoned meat.

"I'm afraid the stew will have to wait, loves. Seems I'll be needed on deck sooner than we thought. The shores of Zy be upon us."

About that time, Finn's voice rang out from the deck.

"All hands on deck!" he shouted. "Prepare for Zy!"

Needless to say, we both ate really fast, cramming as much food down as we could without choking. The belly of the ship grew busy as sailors and soldiers alike grabbed their weapons and swarmed past us. Just as the galley cleared, we put down our plates and followed them out into the morning sun.

We met Finn on the forecastle, looking out at the pale horizon. He turned to greet us with a smile that almost took my breath away. I swallowed before I said hello, trying hard to keep a cool composure about me. What I really wanted to do was kiss him again. I wanted to be alone with him like I had been the night before. Even though I'd resigned myself to reality, that time had not been enough. Did he feel the same way? Was his stomach twisting into knots like mine? Now, as if the passionate tension wasn't unbearable enough, we had this incredible secret between us. I hated that I felt nervous around him, but I loved it all the same.

I glanced over at Kalani a few times, wondering if she could sense what was going on, but then noticed she had her serious eyes focused on the land that had appeared in the sea before us. I felt bad as she stared out at the remains of her land, knowing that her people were trapped there, or even dead. I couldn't imagine the guilt she felt for making it out alive.

The sun was already warming the deck of the ship. The spinner dolphins that had followed us from Everest broke away as we neared the shore. They apparently were more cautious than we were. A low melody rose from the deck below. A sailor hummed the ominous tune, humming louder and louder until another sailor joined in with verse.

From land to deep water, over ocean blue,
We cross to cursed land; evil we pursue.

Come, all you sailors, tell them what you know.
Please listen to us sailors cry, pleading, do not go.

Some shall always rise, some shall always fall,
And some shall always know, death comes for us all.

Come, all you sailors, tell them what you know.
Please listen to us sailors cry, pleading, do not go.

Please listen to us sailors cry, pleading, do not go!

The song left an eerie feeling with me, as the morning sky dulled around us. The water under the ship darkened as we neared the rocky shore of Zy.

The wind turned suddenly harsh, wrapping angrily around the sails. The waves retreating from the island rushed at us with great force, bursting at the bow of the ship. The ocean around us grew unusually restless, swelling with huge black waves in mere moments. The ship creaked and moaned as the bow lifted and slapped against it defiantly.

Many of us stood, staring down at our fate. Only the sound of wind, ocean, and the sailor's tune swept through the ship. Then, suddenly breaking the rhythm of the static noise, was the soft voice of a princess.

"Home," Kalani said as a single golden tear rolled down her cheek.

-14-

WINGED DEMONS

THE DAWN WAS MASKED BY A SMOKY SKY. FINN NOW STOOD firmly with his hands wrapped around the spokes of the large wheel, steering the ship into a deep lagoon on the east side of the island. It wasn't long before we had dropped anchor in the lagoon, which was shadowed by two grey mountains.

Everyone aboard was anxious about stepping into Zy's territory. And here we were, staring down its cursed, blackened shoreline. No one had dared to set foot on the island since the fall of the kingdom. It was said that even the sun never shined on its soil, not since the attack. That myth rang true right now. There wasn't a ray of sunlight to be seen.

Zy had once been a land of great beauty, lush and bountiful with exotic fruits and breathtaking mountains, but all traces of that beauty were gone. The country was completely grey, and beyond the grey was black. The waters of the sea, bright blue further out, appeared black around the island, like tar lapping at its edges. There was a creepy resemblance to Hades. I shivered from the very thought. In the year I had been away, I still had nightmares about that place.

I couldn't deny the fear buried in my gut. None of us knew how strong Erik had become. His father had been alive for centuries, collecting the powers of our people. What had he passed on to his son? What if we were unable to defeat him? How many lives would we lose? I couldn't concentrate on strategy for fearing that we would fail. I finally shook my head, shaking the worries away. This was a battle we had to win at all costs. There had to be a way.

"Pack plenty of food and take as many weapons as you can carry," Finn said, directing our attention to the back of the ship. "Be prepared for anything." He pointed to a pile of weaponry protruding from the mouth of a barrel.

We crowded the barrels, grabbing weapons of choice from the pile. I was able to get my hands on two swords—short in length, but recently sharpened—a bow just my size, and a dozen arrows that were neatly tucked into a leather quiver. Since the blade of Tiger Lily was at my side, I secured both new blades behind my back and strapped the leather quiver between them. I practiced grabbing the swords a few times to make sure they were easy to access, and then I slung the bow over my shoulder. I was ready.

Finn pulled a few men to the side, instructing them to stay behind and guard the ship. The members of the guard were among these men, but the guard clearly stated that staying behind was not an option for them—that they were bound by law to follow the trail of the enemy. This term, enemy, still included me.

We all knew that when this was all over, if I survived, I would be forced to stand before the Senate of Everest. And since I was considered a traitor, there would be little Finn could do for me once I was on trial. Even as king, his opinion could not overrule theirs.

We left the ship by way of long boat. The whole lot of us only filled eight of the boats. There were around eighty of us altogether.

The rigid earth crunched under our feet as we pulled the boats ashore. Oil-soaked torches were passed out to every third soldier, and then a tinder box was passed around to bring them to life. The loud, dancing flames seemed only to soften the darkness that hovered over us.

Every step we took away from the boats could be a step closer to death. The guards insisted on keeping me in their line of sight, inspecting my every move like they would an enemy.

I caught my attention wandering to Finn a few times, but I corrected myself by focusing on the damaged landscape around us. I needed to be alert. Besides the rhythmic crunch of our shoes against the dead earth, not a sound came from the soldiers as we grimly marched ahead, trying to prepare ourselves for the worst.

The ground for the most part was blackened, like coal, and the plants and trees were scalded from fire. It resembled Mars more than it did an island. Every few hours we would come by a patch of grass that had somehow managed to survive. That small amount of color seemed alien to the land now. Kalani's face said it all. The further we journeyed, the more heartbroken she looked.

Nearly half a day passed before we caught sight of the first sign of life. At least, it felt like half a day, though we could only guess due to the lack of sun. It was a black horse—but it wasn't just a horse. Folded neatly to its sides were long black wings, feathered like a bird's.

"Friesian," Finn said. "I'm surprised it didn't migrate to Kenya after the destruction. Unless the fallen are using them. That would explain how they are traveling so quickly." He seemed to be thinking aloud.

It had been almost a decade since I had seen a Friesian. My father had given me my first riding lesson on a visit to the neighboring island of Kenya. We rarely saw them in Everest; the winged creatures preferred the cooler climate of the Northern Islands. Even with the dried mud in its mane, it was still beautiful. Fur dark as the night, with a body that embodied strength and grace. I had almost forgotten how beautiful they were.

I took small steps over to the Friesian, being careful not to spook the creature. "Shhh...shhh...It's alright. We won't hurt you." I kept my voice gentle.

I eased my hand to its neck and stroked backward along its shoulder. The wild creature lifted its muzzle for a moment, flared its nostrils, and then began to extend its wings. We were immediately forced to step back as its wingspan grew to its full potential. The Friesian slapped its front hooves into the mud several times before galloping into flight.

It soared like a bird in the clouded sky, moving its hooves with the same elegant motion as its wings. What was such a graceful creature doing in this dark place?

We pushed forward as soon as the Friesian disappeared in the heavy clouds of grey.

A sickening wind blew over the remains of Zy, causing the dirt to circle around our feet. Everything seemed too quiet, too easy. And everything was—that is, until the peak of Mount Zyon came into view in the distance. That's when all hell broke loose.

It started with one wrong step. I saw three men go down, falling right through the earth without so much as a scream. There was no time for words, or fear even.

As we ran to aid the men who'd fallen out of sight, the culprit grew clear. Booby traps. Deep pits had been dug and filled with wooden spikes sticking vertically from the soil. I regretted looking down the minute I saw their lifeless bodies. The enemy must have stretched a net or a thin fabric over the mouth of the pit and covered it with dirt. My eyes skimmed the perimeter of the hole, catching the points where the fabric had been staked to the ground. That was exactly what they had done. Any of us could have made that fatal step. Any of us.

"May you finally be at peace," Finn whispered.

After a sailor said a few words in the men's honor, Finn instructed us to move forward. That was really all we could do now. The pits were too deep to rescue their brutally damaged bodies. Even though we desired to bury them properly, we had to walk away. We gathered back together and set out with even more caution, checking every step. Only minutes had passed when we heard a deafening screech in the sky, followed by another.

"What is that?" I yelled, clamping my hands over my aching ears.

"*Tei Buo Neh*," Kalani muttered.

"What did she say?"

Finn looked over to me with a worried expression. "Demons of the sky."

They appeared out of the fog, like winged predators on the hunt. And we were their prey.

My jaw literally dropped as I took in the sheer magnitude of their size. There were two of them, with a wingspan double the length of a longboat and a body much larger than that. My rush of fear and adrenaline only intensified as their hellish bodies sliced through the smoky atmosphere and swooped lower, circling closer to our group and becoming clearer in the weak island light.

These beasts had furry gray skin, jaws lined with jagged teeth, and a long spiked tail. Their strange wings connected to a long muscle that acted like an outstretched arm. Tucked underneath their bodies were legs armed with long talons, similar to those of a prehistoric pterosaur. *Demons of the sky.*

They picked off soldiers in seconds, grabbing them with their sharp talons and whisking them away. As soon as the beasts reached a deadly height, they dropped their screaming victims to their deaths, and then circled back to grab another. The few of us with bows filled the dark sky with our arrows. We were lucky enough to bring down one demon in the second attack. It crashed into the hard earth, splattering sickly purple blood onto the dark landscape.

The death of the beast only angered its mate. The furious animal tore through the sky with its long jaw stretched open, grabbing at anyone in sight. It managed to snag one soldier between its gnashing teeth and another between its talons. They disappeared in the smoky atmosphere, appearing only when they plummeted to a horrible death. The beast swooped down again, grabbing another solider between its talons, but this time Finn was close enough to intervene.

In one swing, the blade of his sword clipped one wing, disconnecting the black furry membrane of skin from the muscle. The soldier fell free from the demon's claws just before it crashed into the ground behind us. It let out the same ear-splitting cry from earlier as it flopped against the ground. Several men nearest the screeching beast were stumbling about with blood drizzling from their ears. The unnervingly shrill screech of the flying beast had ruptured their eardrums. I was fortunate enough to have my hands to my ears in time to avoid the same fate. Kalani released an arrow from afar, piercing the throat of the giant bird and silencing the creature for good. Her quick action and accurate aim were truly impressive. I hadn't expected that from a princess.

We lost eleven men total—eleven good men. That brought our fatalities to fourteen. After plucking our arrows from the fallen beasts and taking a moment of silence for the dead, we had no choice but to continue on. The wounded needed water, and their injuries needed to be wrapped and cleaned properly. It seemed cold to leave behind more unburied soldiers, but it had to be done. Finn promised to bury the dead on our journey back. This was a promise that we all hoped we could keep. After all, our fate was still unknown. We left the gruesome battlefield, keeping one eye on the sky in case any other feathered demons were to appear.

15

WHAT IF

WE STOPPED AT THE FIRST SIGN OF RUNNING WATER. THE river was tucked away in a shallow valley that protected a small amount of vegetation. There were trees that had survived the attack, beautiful trees, scarred from fire, but still alive. The water ran clear despite the dust that occasionally blew through the air. One thing to be thankful for, at least. The valley was the first sign that this land might still be worth saving. And from Kalani's smile, I could tell that it was something she'd desperately needed to see.

Everyone was quiet for the first half hour, busy drinking water and thanking the good Lord that they were still alive.

I finished up at the river and wandered to the small hill that shielded the valley from the stretch of land that led to Mount Zyon. There was an eerie glow through the haze, just bright enough to see the outline of the rest of the kingdom. *It must be close to nightfall,* I thought. With the constant shadow over the land, it was impossible to be certain, but the air felt less warm, like night air.

Beyond the valley a scorched country rose in rocky form, ridge after ridge of gray land, till it met the hill known as Mount Zyon. All around this mount were pinnacles and slopes, dark areas of trees, and narrow gorges as far as I could see. The river that quenched our thirst flowed north, cutting through the ridges and around the dark forest, twisting around all obstacles to the base of Zyon. I could only imagine how beautiful this kingdom had been before the fall, before the bright colors of day and lush landscape were stolen from it.

The top of Mount Zyon was flat, with the castle of Zy forming its peak. Its jagged structure was a twisted silhouette shooting into the haze of the sky. It looked to be another half a day's journey from here. It was a bold move for us to camp in the valley, but we were well hidden and protected by the branches of the trees surrounding the river. Finn knew what he was doing.

I walked back down to the river, scattering dragonflies from random patches of grass as I went. I unloaded the weight of my weapons from my back to stretch the muscles that had tightened on my shoulders, and then sat down, listening to the water flow past me. I caught Finn glancing my way.

"You shouldn't have come this far," he said, moving in my direction.

"I'm fine."

He moved behind me and also sat, placing his hands at the nape of my neck. His fingers kneaded my aching muscles, traveling back and forth on my shoulders. My eyes darted all around to make sure we were not being studied by any of the guard. Many of the soldiers had settled slightly away from the river, focusing on cleaning their wounds and setting up a small campsite. The guard had joined them, removing their metal armor and helping see to the wounded. For the moment, only God's eyes were on us.

"You still see me as weak," I said, hoping to stir a response.

"That is where you are wrong." I could hear the smile in his voice. "I see you as a woman carrying a heavier load than most."

I smiled back and unexpectedly shivered from his statement. I'd heard something similar before—from Edmund. I glanced up at the dark sky, my mind wandering to him.

"Are you cold?" Finn asked, placing his jacket around me before I could respond. My thoughts were immediately broken, bringing me back to the present.

I looked around us again to make sure we were still unobserved. "Finn, this has to stop."

"It is only a jacket, Clara."

"Not for me it isn't." I sighed. It was time to tell him that this secret longing needed to end. It *had* to end, but I couldn't stop thinking about him—about how it felt the first time we were torn apart. That miserable emptiness. "Do you ever think about the night everything changed? The night of the renegade?"

"Of course."

"What if none of this had happened? What if it had just been the two of us that night? What if—"

"What if I had kissed you," he said, leaning around me from behind.

I subconsciously bit my lip while I looked into his bright eyes.

"What if…" I whispered.

His fingers slid through my hair, stopping to cup the nape of my neck.

His closeness always quickened the beat of my heart, but this time it was in overdrive, in spite of my fear that we would be seen. I could feel my blood pulse faster than it ever had through my body, pushing away the chill of the night. I knew that this action was hazardous to my heart. I knew we shouldn't. After all, I had barely survived the last kiss.

"I wish for anything that I could be inside your mind, to know every thought you are thinking. I know it must be a beautiful place," he said.

I swallowed. Did he not understand that he was making everything harder? I couldn't shake my yearning for him, not when he was feeding me lines like that. At this rate, I would have to die to get away from my heartache. I'd have to die to leave this longing behind—but even then, wouldn't I love him in death? The feelings that took over my entire being suggested that I would. That I'd always feel this way. I kept my eyes from his in a desperate attempt to keep myself from falling onto his lips.

Kalani came into focus in my peripheral vision, shifting through the soldiers, pushing past the campfire toward the river—toward us.

"This has to stop," I whispered, reminding us both. "No more."

Finn cleared his throat, and the adoring expression left his face. His hands stayed rested on my neck, but his grip loosened as his body tilted back in disappointment. Kalani was getting close. Had our body language given away our secret? Had she sensed the longing in our stares? For all of our sakes, I prayed that she hadn't.

"I need up," I muttered, shrugging his hands and jacket away. My response sounded cold, but I was desperate. If I were cold, then maybe I could finally numb my feelings. I jumped from the ground quickly, hoping to avoid Kalani altogether. I didn't think I had it in me to keep up the false pretense, not now when my thoughts were running wild from Finn's touch.

He stepped in front of me after only a few paces. "Wait. Where are you going?"

"I need some space."

"But, Clara," he said hurriedly. "There's something I wanted to talk to you about...Can we talk, later?"

Kalani was almost close enough for me to make out her perfect cheekbones. This was too close. I could feel my blood pressure increase; the jealously was building, once again.

"I'll be busy," I mumbled. I staggered past him before he had a chance to say another word. I kept my eyes on the gray valley ahead of me, not daring to look back at him. I knew she was with him now. This was how it should be.

The dull valley was filled with moving shadows created by the orange glow of the campfire. My feet were heavy walking around the campsite, keeping my distance from the river—from *them*. I found a spot hidden from the warm firelight, both shadowed with darkness and carpeted in green. I sank down into the softness of the grass until I was surrounded by its out-of-place color.

I felt so far away from everything I knew. Even with Finn standing on the same land, under the same pale moon, he was just as far away as he'd ever been. Was I chasing ghosts? Finn…my father…Was everything and everyone out of my reach? And what was Edmund if not another illusion? Why was this world so cruel? My fingers curled around the cross, the metal warm from the heat of my own skin. The entwined pine needles twinkled under my fingers. The necklace, which had comforted me during my year away from Finn, only agitated me now. I let it fall back to my chest and hurriedly tucked it under my shirt.

Just then, a bearlike figure lumbered through the shadows toward me. I half-stood in surprise and fear, then sat back down with an embarrassed smile as the red of the man's hair came glowing into sight.

"Now why would a pretty lady like yourself be out here all alone?" Red asked.

"I needed to think."

"Don't we all," he stated. "You mind if I sit and think with you, love?"

I sensed where this was going, but I couldn't refuse his company. Not now, when he was the closest thing I had to a friend. I patted the ground, noticing that under my hand, it was bare. Apparently, I'd mindlessly pulled up handfuls of grass in the short time I'd been hiding here. I shot Red the best smile I could muster. As he wiggled down on the earth beside me, he reminded me a little of Maytide.

Now that he was closer, I noticed that strands of his copper hair were braided with small feathers and beads intertwined. There was a large tribal tattoo on his left forearm and a smaller matching one on the side of his neck. Everything about him stood out from the other soldiers.

"So..." he said casually, "what is it we are thinking about?"

I glanced over at him with a disapproving look and simply shrugged. Like I said, saw it coming. I figured ignoring the subject completely was the best policy. So I'd try to get him to talk.

"What's it mean?" I asked, pointing to the bold design on his forearm.

"Joining of two souls," he said. His smile seemed to fade. "It's in memory of my wife, ya see. So that I never forget."

"Oh." The word came out as a simple reaction and seemed inappropriate instantly. "I'm so sorry, Red. What happened to her?"

"Killed by the fallen, long before you were even born."

"Is that why you're here—why you fight?"

"She was my one true love. A thing of beauty, she was. My Roslin, she had the biggest heart, loved everyone, ya know. And they took her from me. Murdered her right before my eyes." His voice cracked. "I fight because no man should have to live through that pain. I fight for the memory of her." There was a long pause as he cleared his throat several times. "She would have liked you, love."

"I'm sure I would have liked her, too."

I leaned into the burly man, slipping my hand over his. We sat like this, accepting each other's silent sympathy, for quite some time. I was glad that he didn't ask about what had been on my mind again. Even though I was sure he already knew. This kindness was exactly what I'd needed. No questions, no judgment, just quiet support.

After we'd watched countless fireflies flicker past us, the quiet came to an end. The distinct sounds of metal clanking and leather squeaking told me the men in camp were donning their body armor. I looked to the river, searching for Finn, but he was no longer there. He was getting the soldiers ready for something.

"We best head back to the group, don't you think? They plan to ride out within the hour."

"Within the hour? I thought we were camping here tonight."

"Finn hopes for a surprise attack. He fears that if we wait, we will lose the advantage, unless we strike tonight."

I nodded in agreement with Finn's decision to push forward, and swiftly moved to my feet.

"That's the spirit," he said.

I felt his hand pat my shoulder as I followed him toward camp.

"Hey, Red?"

"Yes, love?"

"Thanks for the talk."

"Well...I do think I was the one doin' all the talkin'. If we try again, I think I could be quiet long enough to listen to—" I stopped him right there.

"It was what I needed, Red. Really. Thank you."

As we neared the group, Finn had already begun to line up the men.

"What is our head count for those badly injured?" Finn asked.

"Three are wounded badly, sir. Too bad to make it to the castle. They will live to fight another day, but they will certainly slow us down if they continue with us," answered a short, lean man. The man appeared miniature next to the other soldiers.

"Let them know that they will stay at camp."

The soldier slid away from the group and scurried off to a tent set up behind them. There were two soldiers spread out on the ground beside it. I assumed the third was inside. Once the soldier carrying the message rejoined the group, Finn called them all to attention with a quick lifting of his sword.

"Men, listen to me and carry every word I say with you tonight." He spoke with a booming voice that flowed throughout the gray space of the campsite. "This day marks the beginning of a change. Tonight we will storm the mountain of Zyon and we will fight for our families. We will fight for the ones we have lost, and we will fight for our Zyon brothers. For we are all brothers, united in the truth. We are all family! Find courage in what we are to do, for if death is to find us tonight, we will greet it knowing that the blood we lost paid for our freedom from this darkness." He walked the line of soldiers, confident as he spoke. "And in years to come, when our children and our children's children tell our story, they will speak of the battle at Mount Zyon—and they will tell the story of the day we took back our freedom!"

The men responded with loud bursts of cheers. It was a noise that meant they agreed with their leader, they believed in his words, and were ready to follow him wherever he chose to take them.

"We will fight for our brothers! We will fight for our kingdom! We will fight for the truth!" Finn shouted over their roar.

His words quickly became a chant, accompanied by the soul-stirring pounding of their arm guards against their metal chest plates. They were ready. And so was I.

Finn quieted the chant by calling the men back to attention. The camp fell deathly quiet once again.

"Thaddeus, John—you will set up two more tents near the river. This is where Clara and Kalani will stay. You will be guarding them through the night."

Did he just say that I'm staying behind? I could hardly believe that my ears had heard him correctly. I moved swiftly, pushing my way through the line of soldiers.

"I'm going with you," I blurted, my voice risen with agitation.

"You will stay behind with the others."

"No I will not."

"You have come far enough. I will not have you running into any more danger. I need you to stay here. I need to know that you are safe."

'This is my fight, too. You know that!"

"I will search for your father, Clara. You have my word on that."

"You can't just order me to stay! I'm going!"

The soldiers behind me rattled about in their neatly rows, clearly surprised by my blatant refusal to heed Finn's order.

"I figured as much," Finn grumbled before motioning for two members of the guard to break from the line. They stopped next to me, placing a hand on each of my shoulders.

"John and Thaddeus will look after you while I'm gone," Finn repeated. "And they have my permission to restrain you if you attempt an escape. Please don't try."

They will look after me? I was furious that he thought I needed babysitting—that he would do this to me. I was a guardian—I was born to fight!

"I will come back for you when it is safe."

There was no use trying to argue with him. He would only have the guards chain me up, just in case, if I didn't comply. So I decided to let him think that I had. *All I have to do is play along, to act—put on a good performance. I'll find a way to escape. He can't keep me from fighting. He* won't *keep me from fighting,* I thought. *Just play along...*

"You will search every inch of that castle for my father?"

"Of course. If he is there, I will find him."

"Fine," I said. Finn raised an eyebrow at my sudden change of heart, so I tried for a more convincing statement. "If you command me to stay as my *king,* I must obey you. But I am not happy about this."

"Thank you for understanding, Clara. I'll gladly endure your hostility to know you will be safe."

"Humph," I said, storming away from the guards and away from him, back to my secluded spot to pull up more grass and bide my time. He found me just as the troops finished their preparations for departure. He didn't try to kiss me this time, only bent low to whisper one last thing before he led his soldiers into the shadows.

"What if…" he said. And I knew exactly what he meant.

16

STEADFAST

I LEFT MY SHADOWED CORNER AND WATCHED FROM THE FIRE as the man I loved disappeared from the valley with his faithful soldiers. In minutes the sounds of their boots tapping against the rocky landscape vanished as well. I hated that I hadn't gone with them—that I was left here to sit and wait. I understood Finn's motive for having me stay, I just felt that it was a selfish move on his part. It wasn't fair, but I couldn't let my thoughts linger on what was fair and unfair about this. I had to focus on my new task: breaking away from the guards and getting away from the camp unnoticed.

The guard named John walked past me, heading for the trees outside the light of the fire.

"Hey," Thaddeus said quickly. "Where do you think you're going?"

"Since I put up the tents, you take first watch. I've got to take a leak," he shouted back, already stepping into the shadows.

"Sure thing. Don't get yourself lost," Thaddeus responded jokingly.

John mumbled something back, an insult, no doubt, but he had already walked too far for it to be distinguishable.

Thaddeus joined me by the fire, still smirking. He made himself comfortable fairly quick, propping himself against a boulder to take a drink from a silver canister. It was much smaller than the individual ones we kept our supply of water in, so I assumed it was something fermented. I thought this would be a good time to make my move.

As soon as his eyes fell to the fire, I made sure to grab his attention, throwing a flirtatious smile his way.

"It's nice to feel protected," I said. "Especially by such a strong man."

Now, flirting had never been my strong suit. I always felt awkward, and I never knew what to do with my hands, but surprisingly enough, my performance had peaked his interest.

"It's an honor to be trusted with your safety," he said.

He started to grab at the ground, fumbling for an actual water canister near his feet. It was obvious that he was pleased by my remark, flustered even.

I decided to deliver one more line, before the awkwardness settled in.

"Well, since I know I'm in good hands," I said looking up through my lashes, "I should to try to catch some sleep. Wake me if anything changes?" I was surprised at how convincing I sounded.

"Yes, Lady Clara. Certainly. You go get some shut eye. And don't you be worried, you're well protected tonight."

I gave him one more nod as I stood from the fire, and then made my way to the makeshift tent that had been set up by the river. Sneaking away from camp was going to be easier than I'd originally thought. The steady rush of the water would drown out the sounds of my footsteps, and the fast current would carry me where I needed to be. Finn had been naive for thinking he could keep me here, away from the fight, away from my father.

I slid into the tent, leaving a small slit in the fabric behind me. All I had to do was to remain committed to my plan—to watch the solider through the slit for my moment to slip under and out the back of the tent. There was a sudden rustle behind me. I spun around to see Kalani, crouched like a tiger in the shadows.

"What are you doing here?" I strained to whisper, trying to hold back the sudden frustration that had found me.

"I go," she said in a low, stern voice.

"Shhh!" I hissed. I stole a quick peep outside, hoping that Thaddeus and John hadn't heard. Thaddeus was still by the fire, fidgeting with his canteen again, and John was still out of sight.

"You can't," I said. "I'm going alone."

"No." Her eyebrows were crinkled now, her lips stretched tight. "I go."

Her face was unwavering.

It seemed I was not the only one upset about being left behind. She was not going to let me leave without her, which was actually quite admirable.

"Can you swim?" I sighed.

"Yes, yes, swim."

"Fine," I finally agreed. "Be quiet and follow me. Do exactly what I do. You understand?"

She nodded.

In less than a minute we were out of the tent and in the water, riding the current down its curvy, dark path. *Too easy.*

We rode the swift current, cutting through the hills that had hidden the valley. It moved us effortlessly beyond trees and shadows, through ridges and around hurdles. In a way it was nice to have Kalani there with me—after all, she knew this land better than anyone. And I was glad that I wouldn't be going in the castle alone. She was another set of eyes. But I couldn't help wondering if it was a bad idea, that she was now my responsibility to keep safe.

The water flowed faster as it carried us further and further downriver and before long pushed us past the soft yellow glow emanating from the torches of Finn's soldiers trekking through the woodsy territory. It felt good to have something go better than planned. It was about time I had some luck.

Even above the sound of the rushing water, I could hear the steady *thump, thump* of the soldier's march and their quiet voices whispering through the sparse branches of the trees. The wind always carried so many sounds with it. I wished we were marching in formation with them now, instead of floating, fugitives, alone on the river. I think Kalani knew just as I that going rogue would be dangerous, but I was determined to find my father, and I felt that this was something *I* had to do—not Finn, not Edmund…me. It was my fight. Kalani shared the same passion; she wanted the right to fight for what she loved.

After we were several miles ahead of Finn and his soldiers, Kalani started to veer to the right of the river, tugging me along with her.

"Water run fast and dangerous ahead," she said, through shallow breaths. "We walk."

I was already reaping the benefits of having let her come along.

"Alright," I breathed, wading my way to the bank. "You lead the way."

The world around us looked like it came from the depths of a nightmare, more than ever. The trees were completely charcoaled with long, leafless branches that reached out like dark crooked arms. If there were ever such a thing as a ghoul or troll, ghost or headless horseman, it would live in this dark place. Again, I was glad I wasn't alone.

Kalani led us through this maze of dead wildlife, never stopping or turning to look back. As quiet as we tried to be, our footsteps popped and crackled relentlessly against the blackened earth. It was all too creepy. When the colorless land rose to an incline, our pace slowed to a steady walk. We were nearing Mount Zyon.

"We go to...uhh...uhh..." She stuttered for a moment, searching for the right English words. "We go to east of castle wall. We climb."

Climbing was not one of my strengths, but apparently this was our only way in if we wished to stay unnoticed.

I nodded the go-ahead.

The mountain and castle towered before us, with the castle rising just above the tops of the barren trees around us. The east side of the mountain was dry, cracked earth. Before the land had been scorched, it must have been covered in plant life, because now, long, thick vines dangled from its side. I had to tug on a few to be certain, but the dead vines were as strong as rope. Kalani was right to have brought us here.

We scaled the mountain, side by side, swinging from one available vine to the next. The first eight or so yards were relatively easy, but then the vines seemed to spread further apart.

As the ground below us appeared more distant and the tops of the trees became clearer, we realized that we'd have to use the cracks in the rock to climb the last few yards to the top. I glanced over to check on Kalani. She clung tightly to the last available vine near her.

I examined the face of the mountain above us, pinpointing the exact locations of the cracks, holes, and protrusions from the earth. There was a small horizontal edge just barely within my reach, two holes the size of baseballs about three feet above that, and then the stump of a tree that stuck out from the surface a few feet over the two holes. If I could get there, I could probably reach the last vine hanging from the top. Then, I could lower something down to pull Kalani the rest of the way up. If I didn't fall to my death first, that is.

At this point, I had forbidden myself to look down. There were only a few more yards to go. I just had to find support with my hands and feet, and I needed to trust my balance and my own strength. *I can do this.*

"Can you reach that vine?" I whispered, using my elbow to point to a long vine dangling between the two of us.

With a hesitant nod, she swung her weight so that she inched closer and closer to the vine. In seconds, she had the second vine in her hand.

"Good," I said. "Now swing it to me."

She carefully gauged the distance between us before swinging the vine right to me. I could tell that she was curious as to what I was doing. As I rolled up the vine one handed, fishing for the end, I explained to her my hopeful plan.

"I'll tie the end of this vine to my arm and climb to the top. Then, when I get to the top, I'll hold the end while you climb up. You can swing over to it again, right?"

She nodded her head, looking terrified, but eagerly agreeing with the only plan we had.

I found the very end of the vine and secured it to my arm. Step one.

Then, I stretched my right arm as high as I could until I felt the crack in the rock. It was about two inches deep. After mentally encouraging myself, I shoved my right hand into the slit and released my safe grip. My left hand quickly found its way to the same edge as my feet searched for footing below me. My breathing quickened and the sound of my heartbeat throbbed in my ears, but I kept reassuring myself that everything was fine.

I started to feel my weight pull at my arms; I needed to move fast before my arms and fingers gave out. This time, I reached with my left hand, feeling for one of the two baseball-shaped holes. As soon as I found it, I locked my fingers down and reached for the one next to it with my right hand. Got it! *Okay, this isn't so bad. You're almost there...*

My shoes scraped against the rock, still in pursuit of a foothold, while I stretched for the end of the log above me. My hand couldn't seem to find it, even though I knew it was there. My other hand ached, clinging to only inches of rock, and the muscles in my arm began to quiver.

"Go left," Kalani said in a worried tone.

I moved my fingers so that they eagerly explored left of where I'd originally been searching. I wasn't sure how much longer I could hold myself up. *Come on...come on...*

"Up, up," she continued to coach. "Almost."

And just as a bead of sweat rolled down my neck, my hand wrapped around the log. I threw my second hand up to meet it, and then took a moment to breathe. The last vine dangled only a foot above my hands. This was no place to rest; I was almost to the top.

Straining against the total muscle exhaustion in my shaking arms, I heaved my body upwards, *just* far enough to grab the final vine. With one swift motion, I wrapped the sturdy vine around my hand and pulled my way to the top of the mountain. *Safe.*

Once I rolled safely onto flat land, I retied the end of the vine so that it looped around my waist instead of my wrist. Even though Kalani was probably barely over a hundred pounds, I knew this would help steady her weight as she climbed. I looked over the edge and motioned for her to come. She had to climb to the top of the vine she'd been holding on to, and then jump over to the one that I had anchored.

When both her hands were on the vine, I felt myself slide forward under her weight. I quickly bent my knees, planted my feet, and walked back to pull out the slack. I couldn't see over the edge anymore, but from the tension in the vine, I knew she was getting closer to the top. I only hoped that the vine wouldn't give way before then. The sweat was building on my forehead again. I don't think a single breath made it in or out of my lungs until I saw the top of her golden hair shimmer at the edge.

Sometime in between running to her and pulling her up, I started breathing again. We'd both made it to the top. I could only hope there would be a different path, leaving the castle.

Voices from overhead forced us to duck under the skeleton of a bush sitting a few feet from the ledge. I looked between the leafless branches to take note of the stone barrier in front of us. The voices came from the top of the wall. One was very deep and raspy, sounding more like a growl than a voice. A shadow walker. The other voice was clear and precise, a beautiful sound to the ears. A fallen one. Both were our enemy.

"Is there a way in?" I whispered, still keeping my body close to the ground.

"Yes, way in. Look?" Her long narrow finger pointed to a dark space on the bottom portion of the wall. "See?"

"There?" I squinted, trying to see how this was our way in.

The enemy finally disappeared into a tower on the north side of the barrier wall, giving us the freedom to sprint for this so-called opening. Kalani took off first, darting to the area she had pointed out. I quietly followed. When we stood directly in front of the wall, I saw a hole the size of my fist in the barrier and deep cracks between four of the stones around it. These stones had been moved before. I wondered if this had been the path my father had chosen to help Kalani and the elders escape during the attack. That would explain how she knew we could safely scale the east side of the mountain.

We both placed our palms against the first rectangular stone, pushing it forward until it gently slipped from the wall. It was low enough to the ground that only a soft thud sounded as it hit. After pausing for a moment to make sure no one charged out into the night, we did the same with the remaining stones. There were three more soft thuds as each fell next to the first freed stone.

The hole we'd created was less than a yard wide, but it was still big enough for us to crawl through. I wiggled through first, keeping my eyes and ears alert for any sign of the enemy. After we both stood inside the barrier wall, we heaved the stones back into place, covering our tracks. We would have to be invisible if we wanted to survive this; it was our only chance.

Most of the towers and outerworks on the south side of the castle had been destroyed in the attack, which would give us the upper hand when Finn arrived with his soldiers. From the lack of men stationed on the tops of the outer barrier—I'd counted only three more of the enemy facing the north and south sides—Erik hadn't feared an attack on his fortress. He probably thought no one would dare stand up to him and his army, or maybe he believed that Everest was still unaware of his plans.

The cold, grey stone walls seemed taller now that we were inside them. There were two square towers and two round towers that made up the corners of the castle before us. The square towers were open on top like the ones on the barrier wall, but the round towers were roofed with grey tile. The only entrances through the courtyard were the doors to these towers and a dark archway straight ahead.

As I surveyed the courtyard, Kalani tapped me on the shoulder and directed my gaze to the top of the outer wall.

"I cover you," she said.

I assumed that Kalani didn't have much combat experience, because a princess was never expected to fight. So other than the encounter with the shadow walkers, I didn't think she'd ever experienced battle, but she had a bow and a set of arrows, and she was a pretty decent shot from what I'd witnessed. That was good enough for me. A pair of eyes in the sky was an excellent plan. And it seemed to be the safest route for the both of us.

"Okay." I nodded. "Where do I go from here?"

She pointed to the archway at the end of the courtyard. "Stairs," she said.

"Through there?" The darkness surrounding the archway didn't look promising from where we stood.

"*Boi ess,*" she started to say but corrected herself with the translation. "Yes, yes. Go there. Right stairs go to chapel. You see door in chapel. Door go to long hallway. You see great hall from above."

Getting strategic directions from someone who spoke broken English had its flaws, but at least she was giving me some insight on what to expect.

"So, go through the arch and take the stairs on the right, go through the chapel, and follow the hallway until I see the great hall?"

"Yes, yes." She quickly threw an arm around me and lightly squeezed. "Clara, my sister...be safe."

Why did she have to call me her sister? It only made me feel worse about the feelings for Finn that I tried desperately to hide. This whole time I'd been learning to despise her for something that really wasn't her fault. How could I blame her for being attracted to Finn? He was irresistible—I could verify that. And our two kingdoms had come to the agreement that they should wed, not her. *Ugh...Why does she have to be nice, too?*

"You, too. Be safe, that is." I halfway hugged her back before we both took off in different directions.

I ran along the outer walls, then slipped through the dim archway, hopefully unnoticed.

I was inside. There were roars of laughter and cheering coming from deep within the castle. The sound echoed, bouncing from the walls.

In my first few steps inside, I came across a motionless body, bent over an empty bottle of spirits. Passed out drunk, apparently. I lightly tapped his shoulder, accidentally tipping the unconscious man completely over in the process. His only reaction to this was to snore, loudly. I figured his cloak would help me to blend in, so my hands flew to work, pulling the dark brown cloak from the drunk. Flinging it over my shoulders, I took off in search of the stairs.

I made my way down the empty hall, passing doors and passageways on each side of me, until I came to a set of stairs on my right. There was very little light in the stairway, but I managed to find my way up to the chapel without tripping. It was quite an accomplishment, since several steps had been missing.

I entered the chapel with caution, expecting to come across someone or something, but there was still no sign of the enemy. The chapel was dimly lit and desolate like the entry of the castle, but the damage done to such a sacred place shook me to my core. Broken pieces of stained glass lay across the floor, a large cross had been torn from the wall, and the candlesticks and wooden chalices were crushed, lying among a bed of ripped scrolls. I felt the familiar burn in my eyes, warning me to stay strong.

My feet crunched against the glass as I shuffled through. I had to stay focused. *Focus. One thing at a time*, I told myself. *Find the door.*

I tried my best to look past all the destruction, inspecting every corner of the chapel until I finally spied a metal door.

I nearly jumped to it, eager to move ahead and out of this tragic room, but I had to clear the floor of debris so that I could pull it open. While I slowly opened the creaking door with one hand, my other rested on the hilt of my sword.

Another seemingly empty hall was on the other side of the door. Where was everyone? So far, everything had been too easy. The cheering was louder in this hallway; the floor under my feet vibrated from the sound. And there was a clearly rotten smell in the air. I prepared myself to be met with a shadow walker at any minute.

I followed the noise and sickening smell, turning a corner to find the source of all the noise. This passageway opened up, wrapping around the great hall like a balcony in a grand theater. I kept in the shadows, hiding behind a column while looking down at the great hall below. Every square inch of the hall was filled with fallen ones and shadow walkers, hundreds of them, shouting and pushing to make bets on some fight.

The great hall had been turned into something like a coliseum. The entire roof was missing, left open to the night air, and stone seating had been fashioned around the walls, where men and woman sat elbow to elbow encouraging the brawl. I noted the weaponry hanging behind them. Crossbows, spears, clubs, and even tridents covered the walls.

A second balcony, below mine, was lined with more spectators, throwing random bits of trash down into the crowd. Some seemed to be cheerful while others were plain angry.

Erik sat at the front of the great hall in a large throne that overlooked the fight. Even from here, I could see an evil grin plastered across his face. Next to him in the shadows of his throne stood Sienna, the bushy-haired red head I remembered so vividly from the year before. She looked more like a belly dancer now, wearing a gold sequined bra and a wide golden belt that held up a thin red skirt. She, along with Erik, seemed glued to the fight.

My stomach twisted at first, when I realized what was going on, and then my ears burned from the anger boiling in my blood. This fight wasn't a fight at all. It was a shadow walker beating a helpless man, a man in chains. The captive was skin and bones, barely capable of standing. Across the forehead of this fragile man were the same stripes I'd seen painted on the elders. He was a Zyon.

More shouts rang out from all around as the shadow walker pummeled this defenseless captive within an inch of his life.

Erik's hand rose slightly from the arm of his throne, and a hush fell across the crowd. The shadow walker hovered over the defeated man, waiting for Erik's signal to give the final blow.

"Join us," Erik said. "Join my army, and the pain you know will cease to exist."

"Never!" The man's voice quivered from pain, but it rang with defiance. I bit my lip to keep from screaming as I searched frantically for a way to save the helpless man.

"Then meet your death, just as the Zyons before you," he said, nodding to the shadow walker.

My eyes darted around the hall again, desperately trying to find a way to get down there—but I couldn't find anything in my frantic search. The long arms of the shadow walker rose, gripping a spiked club high above the captive's head. The faithful Zyon's voice rose in passionate prayer, spoken in the language of his people, becoming louder with each word. The shadow walker shifted the club in his hands as he adjusted his aim. I began to run down the hall, looking for a way to stop the horror, and then the prayers of the Zyon fell quiet. It was too late. I looked down into the evil mob, witnessing the residue of life leave the prisoner's body.

The crowd went wild. I almost threw up.

I swallowed, trying hard to clear the knot in my throat and subdue the nauseous feeling in my stomach. I had seen blood before—I had seen men die before. But to watch a crowd cheer as a man was killed in cold blood, killed for sport, was something no one could be prepared to see. This was something nightmares were made of.

The mob hushed for a moment when Erik stood to make an announcement.

"Now for the main event," he said. "Bring out the traitor!"

I peered over the edge again, nervous to see who was next. The crowd parted as a man was forced forward to the center of the makeshift arena. He came from the side underneath the balcony where I stood; all I could see was a long black frock hanging sleek against his back. And then he spoke.

"You will fall," said the man, his voice filled with certainty. It was the strong, low tone that gave him away. They had Edmund. No one in the crowd interrupted him as he continued. "Whether I live or die, your reign will end. And how sweet that day will be. The people will rejoice over your death."

No! No, no, no, no. How did this happen? I couldn't watch them kill him. There had to be a way to get down there. I took off running down the passageway, until a figure stepped out from a hallway.

"Are you enjoying the games?" The voice was smug, just like it had always been. There was no doubting who it was.

"Get out of my way, Lydia," I hissed, ripping my sword from its metal sheath.

She smirked, pleased at my annoyance. "Erik really knows how to put on a good show, don't you think? I personally enjoy it when they beg for their sad, useless life."

I ignored her remark, hearing a shuffle behind me, accompanied by a rotten stench in the air. A shadow walker was practically upon me.

I spun, bringing my blade around just in time to slice through the creature's midsection. For any human or fallen one, it would have been a fatal blow, but to kill a shadow walker, I needed fire. Something I didn't have. The unharmed creature ripped my weapon from my hand and backhanded me across the face. The force of the blow drove me straight to my knees.

"Search her for other weapons," Lydia instructed, leaning down to rip my pendant from my neck. "Let's take her to Erik. He'll be pleased to see she has come to us."

Another shadow walker, just as tall and ugly as the first, stripped me of my remaining weapons and then forced me back to my feet. He grumbled a reply to Lydia's instruction before each grabbed one of my arms. I was immediately dragged forward down a dark hall. Behind us, the noise from the arena intensified, making the stairs under our feet shake. I tried hard to keep a calm composure, but my pulse pounded in my cheek where the shadow walker had struck, and my stomach churned, barely keeping down my last meal.

The moment we entered the great hall, the dirty stench of the crowd mixed with the blood of the slain further assaulted my senses. I felt tugs against my hair and clothes as Erik's monsters pushed me through screaming men and women, to the clearing.

Edmund was in the middle of the arena, bent over and panting heavily, when I neared. His mask and clothing were now splattered with his own blood, but he still managed to find the strength to stand. When his head tilted up, and he discovered my arrival, I could see the shock and anger blaze to life in his eyes.

"What are you doing here?" he shouted. "I told you to stay away from this place! You shouldn't be here!"

I had no response. I had obviously failed miserably in rescuing him, in finding my father, and in saving the Zyons. My capture only worsened the matter. And now, I'd given Erik what he wanted, what he needed for the dark side of the prophecy to come true—me.

Erik stood in the background, signaling the shadow walkers to move from the arena. The creatures released my arms, allowing the blood to flow to my hands once again. Edmund was quick to shove his own guard away, then move across the arena to me.

I reached out, finding comfort in his closeness. His arm closed around my shoulders, and I could feel his body quiver with each heavy breath. His wounds were hidden underneath his heavy clothing, but it was obvious that he was in severe pain.

"Stay behind me," he said through another weighted breath. "And keep your eyes from his."

"Edmund, I'm sorry—" I whispered, but my apology was cut short.

"Well, it looks like tonight we are all in for a treat!" Erik arrogantly stepped from the platform, parting the mob as he walked across the arena to where we stood.

With an effortless flip of Erik's wrist, an unseen force seized Edmund. I grabbed his arm, trying to keep him on his feet as he struggled with the dark magic Erik used against him, but my efforts failed. Edmund's knees shook, his arms tightened, his teeth clenched, the veins on his neck bulged, until this invisible enemy knocked him to the stone floor. It was the same pressure technique Victor had used in Hades. Erik was stronger than before; he had inherited his father's dark power.

Erik threw a rope to the floor. It slithered over to Edmund as if it had the body of a snake and knotted itself around his wrists. I reached to help him, but a force of cold air pushed me away. My feet slid across the floor until I was yards away from him.

A beastly expression formed on the face of the dark prince as he neared. I saw his hand clench, and my legs became weighted to the floor. His hand unclenched and made a circular motion in the air, causing my arms to freeze by my sides. My limbs were locked into place, as if cold chains had wrapped around my entire body. I grunted, fighting against the pressure surrounding me. I couldn't move.

I kept my eyes on the ground, focusing on staying calm and keeping my guard up. Erik's snakeskin boots clicked against the floor as he circled to inspect me.

"Leave her alone!" Edmund demanded, fighting against the rope and the force that held him to the floor.

A fearful chill ran through me. *Stay strong,* I reminded myself. *Fight him. Don't let him in.* He whipped the brown cloak from my shoulders and threw it to the floor. I noticed some crazy, half-mad woman scramble to grab it. I continued to search my mind for courage and strength, hoping to find it before I had to speak.

"I told you once that it would be easier if we were friends, if you would let go," he said, sliding his hand down the length of my arm. "But you didn't listen."

I moved my head back and forth, refraining from looking into his eyes. I wanted to scream at him, but the cold air squeezing at me made it hard to breathe.

"Come to me now, and we shall build the darkest of empires," he said.

His hands tilted my face upward. I caught a glimpse of his black eyes and devilish grin before I squeezed my own eyes shut. His voice snaked its way into my mind. *Come to me, Clarabella. Together we will have everything. Come to me, and we will rule as gods of the darkness.*

The familiar pull of his gift moved toward my subconscious, but I fought against it. He might be able to control my body momentarily, but not my mind—never again would he have that kind of power. I was no longer a moth drawn toward a flame. Faith and knowledge had strengthened the weak girl that had once stood before him. I had been transformed, my mind renewed, so that I could fight against him. I was born to fight—born to stand up for what was good. I was born to fight for the will of God. *I will fight, until my last breath.*

I opened my eyes and spit in the face of the monster before me, interrupting the blasphemous thoughts he pushed in my mind.

"No! Never will I join you." His voice in my subconscious disappeared completely.

The stunned crowd waited silently for Erik's response to my disobedience.

"Stupid girl! You forget who you are dealing with!"

"I know exactly who I'm dealing with! You don't scare me!"

"Then you have a lesson to learn!"

He signaled the creatures that had dragged me in, but was interrupted by Lydia.

"Let me rough her up," she pleaded. "I've been dying to get my hands on her."

"Fine," he said. "Entertain me—show her pain. Make her bleed her guardian blood. Leave her only enough to keep her alive. I want to hear her beg for me."

Edmund was pulled out of the arena by two of the largest shadow walkers I had ever seen. He managed to free his fists long enough to shove one creature and punch another, but this only angered them. Edmund fought to get to me. He shouted my name just as one of the creatures slammed the hilt of its weapon against Edmund's head. He slumped over, immediately unconscious from the blow.

"Edmund." My lips moved, but I couldn't speak. *Please, wake up,* I thought. *Don't let them kill you.*

"Take him to the tower and secure him to the rack," ordered Erik. "Make him as uncomfortable as possible, but leave the best for last. I want to be there when his bones break."

The rack. This was a device for torture. The victim's arms and legs were tied to the top and bottom of a wooden frame. With a twist of a handle, every joint in their body would be pulled apart. Torture such as this was not allowed in Everest or in any of our allied kingdoms for a good reason. It was beyond cruel, and no one ever survived.

I felt sick again. I had failed in every way. Everything had gone from bad to worse. Our only hope rested on an invasion. Where were Finn and his troops? And where was Kalani?

The force of the invisible chains released me as Erik rejoined Sienna at his throne. I was left alone with Lydia, now. I surveyed the arena as thoroughly as I could, trying to spot something that might be useful as a weapon. My eyes stopped on a fallen one, standing to the left of me. He had two sabers tucked neatly away by his side. *Bingo.* There were twenty-one stones that made up the floor between those sabers and me, each stone measuring a little less than a foot in length. With a little strategy and sleight of hand, those sabers would be mine.

"I've been waiting a long time for this," Lydia said, smiling to reveal all of her teeth.

She began to circle me, giving me the perfect opportunity to gradually move toward my weapons. She made the rookie's mistake of carelessly lunging forward, putting all of her weight into her swing instead of grounding her right foot. I dropped my left shoulder, causing the tip of her sword to slice through thin air. Her weight caused her to stumble, leaving her chest completely unprotected. I gave her a direct kick to the ribs, just a little something to say hello. Anyway, it gave me enough time to reach around and swipe the sabers from the naive onlooker.

"You're going to pay for that," she said, coughing and shrugging her embarrassment away.

"Hardly," I replied as I twirled my newfound weapons.

"You think you can fight me?" Lydia chuckled. "You were always overly ambitious. It's sad really."

"And you were always the weak underachiever," I said. "I guess that explains your turn to evil."

"Let me share a little secret," she said dramatically, reaching for a sword held by a shadow walker. "You haven't lived until you've chosen to be bad."

We circled one another, moving our weapons to intimidate. I counted the steps as I taunted her, feeling up the size of the entire arena. *Thirty-four steps.* I created a mental circle with the circumference of eleven steps, which surrounded her, just as my father had taught me to do so long ago. If she moved, the circle moved, but nothing in that circle would get by me.

The hilt of the two sabers I clutched had now warmed from the heat of my hands. I was ready.

"I enjoyed my time in your world, watching you struggle day after day. It almost seemed unfair how pathetic you were. You'll always be weak and pathetic," she said. "Tell me, do you get that from your mother or your father?"

She had gone too far. The desire to destroy her ripped through me, fueling my thirst for revenge. I lunged, slicing the sword in my right hand toward her head. She blocked, but not fast enough to keep the tip of my left sword from grazing her cheek. I knew that I had missed my opening to behead her, but I certainly had given her something to think about.

"Bitch!" she screamed as she backed away.

"I think that will scar nicely, don't you?" I smirked.

She came at me full swing. The sword in my left hand stopped her blade, sliding down the full length of the steel, and then the blade from my right hand forced her sword away.

"It's funny how Erik has you down here, fighting his battles for him. Especially since you're so sloppy with your weapons."

We slowly began circling each other again. I could feel her anger building.

"What are you now, anyway? Slave to the damned?" I said. "I don't know if anyone has ever told you, but there's not much of a future in that."

I gripped the hilt of each sword, knowing that her rage would attack me at any moment. And that's what I wanted. Her rage would cloud her judgment, prompting her to strike quickly and carelessly. This would give me the upper hand.

She charged straight at me with her steel held high, but just before her thirteenth step, she tumbled forward and hit the stone floor with a hard thump. She didn't move.

The entire arena fell quiet for a moment, then crescendoed in a buzz of confused and curious conversation. No one seemed to know why she was lying still against the floor. Not even me.

At first I thought this was a strange tactic of hers. Pretending to be incapacitated. She always did love dramatics. But then I saw all the blood.

Crimson encircled her body, seeping through her blouse and running into her perfectly highlighted hair. Her skin was flushed—her eyes glazed. An arrow protruded from the side of her thin body. *An arrow? Has Kalani come to my rescue?* I glanced to the balcony but saw only the silhouettes of the cloaked fallen and shadow walkers.

A fallen soldier entered the arena, marching straight to Lydia. He pulled the arrow from her side and held it high so that Erik and the crowd could see the cause of her destruction.

"Seize her!" Erik demanded, taking on a more defensive approach. It was now apparent that I was not the only one who'd secretly entered his fortress. "Search the grounds for others!"

I swiftly slid to the floor next to Lydia and grabbed my pendant from her pocket before being thrown into the arms of a shadow walker.

Suddenly, arrows rained down from the balconies of the hall, injuring dozens in the assembly. I looked up just in time to see faces that I knew, Kalani, Red and Dodger, and many other soldiers, revealing themselves to the unsuspecting enemy. They had managed to infiltrate the castle, just as Kalani and I had.

As the shadow walker dragged me across the floor, more of Finn's soldiers rushed around the balconies. The sound of steel against steel rang down into the great hall.

Another group came charging down the stairs and through archways into the hall. I saw Finn leading them, slashing through the angry mob of fallen, fighting his way to get to me. Drawn blades of fire circulated the arena, quickly heating the air, while the ash from the slain creatures drifted like snow. Bodies were hurled from the balconies as more flaming arrows flew down. Small fires erupted throughout the place, catching on shredded curtains and debris. It was smoky chaos.

Through the smoke, I noticed a rope drop from the ledge of the second-story balcony. Red's husky figure slid down the length of the rope, pounding dark soldiers as he made his way to the ground. He landed at the front of the hall and was immediately bombarded by the shadow walkers that guarded the platform where Erik stood in safety.

I'd never noticed just how strong Red was, until this moment. He looked like a Viking, taking out creatures two at a time. He was closing in on us quickly—he was almost to me. Almost.

The enemy took notice, swarming him like a street gang. They had been ordered to take me to Erik, and they were prepared to fight off anyone who stood in their way.

There was a lot of shuffling around me, briefly blocking Red from my line of sight, but I pulled and tugged until I spotted him again.

He was angrier than ever, lashing out at the shadow walkers that had gathered around him, but now he was without his fiery sword. He yanked an axe from the leather belt around his waist, bravely readying himself for the personal attack to come.

Without fire, he had no chance.

One of the boxy creatures twirled a spear in its crusty hands, then aimed and flung it, launching the weapon directly into Red's left shoulder. Red countered quickly, throwing his last weapon into the creature's neck, but his axe was useless without fire.

I screamed so loud that my throat burned, but my scream couldn't stop what was happening right before my eyes. The shadow walker pulled the axe from its neck, dropping it to the floor, and then made his way to Red. The irritated creature broke the spear projecting from Red's shoulder and forced the jagged end upward into his chest. Red continued to lash at the beast even as his own blood stained his lips crimson.

"Nooo!" I cried out again.

I fought against two creatures, jabbing my fists and elbows into their dry flesh. It was like punching hard clay. My knuckles stung and dripped with blood, but I didn't stop punching.

Red fell to the ground. His hand reached for me once. Then he was gone.

A second surge of energy filled the castle as freed Zyons swarmed the arena. Their dark skin beamed with sweat and pre-inflicted wounds, and the similar striped markings I'd seen on the faces of the elders made them easily recognizable as our allies. They brought down the fallen with clubs, stakes, and weapons gathered from the wall while Finn's soldiers concentrated on taking down the shadow walkers with fire. Soldiers fell left and right from both armies, but with the help of the Zyons, we were noticeably weakening the enemy.

Finn still slashed his way forward across the hall while his eyes tracked my ever-changing position.

I could hear Erik shouting instructions from time to time, telling his dark soldiers what to do, but it was clear that Finn had the better strategy for every move Erik's soldiers made. Two large shadow walkers stayed fixed around Erik, guarding him from any possible attack. Two other creatures continued to keep me restrained and guarded like a prized possession. I had become exhausted from fighting against the creatures, but I kept at it, hoping their harsh grip might eventually loosen from my arms.

Nothing seemed to slow Finn down. He was angry, filled with a passion to kill those who'd killed the ones he loved, but he didn't seem to let this anger weigh him down or fog his line of sight. No, he knew exactly what he was doing. His sword never stopped moving; he dodged spears and sharp blades, traveling confidently, daring the world to stop him. It was apparent that no one could and no one would. Not until he got what he wanted.

When he had finally won his way to the front of the hall and discovered Red's lifeless body lying at the foot of the platform, his fierceness amplified to the extreme. His eyes revealed the same intense hatred that he had the night his mother and brother were murdered.

Like a relentless superhero, he charged up the stairs of the platform, threatening Erik as he approached.

"You will die for all that you have done!" he yelled. "Release her, and I might spare you the slow, painful death you deserve."

Erik bellowed a laugh. "You cannot kill me. I am much too powerful for you," he responded, still laughing. "If anything, you should be begging me to be gentle with your girl, because after I kill you, she's mine to do with as I please. And there's a lot I plan to do with her."

"Enough!"

Finn charged, dropping to his knees to slide underneath the wide blade of one of the creatures that was guarding Erik. Before the creature had time to reposition its sword, Finn twirled his blade through its side, turning it into a pile of dirt on the podium floor. The second creature threw a spiked club at Finn's head, but he ducked with inches to spare. The creature growled and then pulled out another weapon, a long crooked sword, to challenge Finn.

As soon as the creature made the first strike at Finn, Erik shouted a command in a language that I assumed only the shadow walkers understood. My two guards dragged me between them to the shadows of the wall behind us. With a motion of his hand, Erik magically opened a secret passage in the stone, revealing a narrow tunnel, and then proceeded to inch his way to me.

All of us knew the danger if Erik managed to escape with me. And I knew that whatever happened, I had to make sure that I didn't go with him. I knew this very well might be the death I was warned about. This might be the day that I died to save this world from further destruction. Someone had to keep me from leaving, even if it meant killing me. I had to be prepared.

"Finn!" I screamed.

Finn rammed his shoulder into the large creature fighting him, throwing its heavy weight off balance. In seconds, the end of Finn's sword plowed into its gut. The shadow walker fell to its knees, spilling sand from the puncture, until it disappeared into the air like the others before it.

Erik looked somewhat surprised that Finn was able to bring down two of his largest guards so quickly. He had underestimated his ability to fight. Erik looked at me, studying the distance between us. He then directed his attention to Finn, staring down the path between them in an effort to influence him with his gift. I could only imagine what Finn was hearing in his head.

"Stand down," Erik commanded. "Leave her to me. That is what *you* want."

Erik's eyes were intense as he tried to work his dark magic, but Finn was much too strong to fall victim to his power of persuasion.

Finn nearly flew to my side, breaking the triangular formation that had shaped between the two of us and Erik. His sharp blade of fire seared off the arms of both of my shadow walkers so speedily that the sudden release of their grip almost caused me to collapse. Their complete destruction came only seconds later. Erik was not pleased.

Finn forced me back, placing his body between me and Erik, just as Edmund had done in the arena.

"I must admit, you're better than I thought, mortal," Erik confessed. "Now, you must fight me."

Erik drew the blade of Tiger Lily for the first time, pointing it directly at me. "Let's see if you're willing to die for her, shall we?"

I noticed Finn's knuckles tighten around his hilt, channeling his fury into the blade. All my muscles tensed as I watched him accept the challenge. No one knew just how powerful Erik had become, but I knew he wouldn't play fair. This felt like a bad idea.

"Finn," I muttered, and then looked to Erik. "Please don't do this."

"It seems she has little faith in you making it out alive," Erik nagged. "Bow out gracefully. Let me take her, and I'll see that you live another day. That's more than a fair proposition."

"I did not come here to negotiate," Finn snarled. His shoulders squared as he paced in front of me. "You will never have her."

I'm not sure whose blade struck first, only that steel clashed and sparks flew. Finn's eyes narrowed with each lunge and each counter, locked in deep concentration.

I watched warily, wondering if Erik was the reason for this steely concentration. Was he still trying to get inside Finn's head? Would his power weaken Finn's strategy in the fight?

The fight came to a standstill, both swords pressed heavily against each other. The steel scraped, sliding back and forth, but neither opponent was able to move. The men's feet were planted; their faces were twin masks of determination and rage. Sienna appeared out of the depths of the podium, moving slowly into the light. Her focus was tied to Erik the way mine was on Finn. With their swords crossed, this had become a battle of strength rather than skill or agility. And it seemed that their strength was equally great.

Gradually, Finn pushed Erik's blade, so that it tilted slightly down. Then in one quick motion, he swiveled to strike Erik's side. Dark blood oozed from the wound; the strike had gone fairly deep. Erik shuffled back, furious, but weakening. Sienna ran to him, whispering something in his ear. He nodded, still holding his sword in an angle of attack.

She stepped away from him and raised her hands high above her head. Erik grinned as Sienna's bright red hair whipped around in a sudden whirlwind that had sprung from nowhere, turning her curls into waves of fire. The warmth of the room intensified to a stifling degree, while a ball of fire appeared in the open sky of the room. She had summoned fire—an ability she had been hiding all along. *Why did she have a gift?* The battle below paused as everyone's eyes shot to the sky.

A winged horse formed from the fire, an animated inferno in the night air. It swooped down through the hole of the roof, bringing a breeze in the new heat wave. The blazing horse landed on the platform, separating Finn and me from Erik. Rings of smoke shot angrily from the animal's muzzle as the dark prince mounted. Erik realized that even his power was weak against us—against Finn in combat. He was a coward; he was running away from the fight.

Erik mounted the flaming horse, pulling Sienna behind him.

"Kill them—kill my entire army! I'll make thousands more!" he yelled to Finn. "Clara will never be safe from me. I will come for her—she will be mine. And your world will fall to darkness deeper than you can comprehend."

The horse reared back, lengthened its long wings in the air, and then took to the sky. All we could do was watch helplessly as Erik, Sienna, and the blade of Tiger Lily flew away on the wings of fire.

Finn dropped his weapon to wrap his arms around me, cradling me close.

"If anything had happened to you..." he whispered.

"But it didn't."

I wanted to spend the rest of my life in those arms, I wanted to tell him how happy I was to be there with him, but I couldn't give in to that desire, not again. I stepped out of his embrace, trying to keep myself from showing too much emotion.

"Go," I said. "The fight isn't over. Lead them to victory."

Finn stood dazed for a moment, staring deeply into my eyes with the same questioning look I had seen the last time I pushed him away. I hated acting this way towards him, but it was the only way. I knew my place, and so did he. He just needed to be reminded.

He nodded, reluctantly. "Stay here," he said.

I watched him straighten, then leap down from the platform, jumping back into fight mode.

My eyes scanned over the hundreds of faces, watching as our enemy was gradually destroyed. Dodger and another soldier had already pulled Red from the floor, resting him against the wall so that his body would go undisturbed. These acts of loyalty made me want to run back into Finn's arms and confess everything I felt for him, and how deeply. But that was what a close encounter with death did to a person: it always gave time meaning.

Just below the platform, to my right, one of Finn's soldiers was knocked off his feet. The soldier collapsed from a side injury, dropping his sword in a mangle of debris. The poor man was scrambling to find it as a dark soldier neared. I had to do something.

Grabbing an abandoned sword from the stairs of the platform, I charged at the enemy in hopes that I would direct his attention away from the injured soldier.

Our blades collided with a loud clash, sending vibrations to the hilt of my sword. I assessed his size and strength during that first blow. This fallen one was quite large, towering several feet above me with a great force behind his steel.

Within seconds, he was pounding his sword into mine, over and over. I stumbled from the force of his advance before recovering enough to properly counter his attack.

I sidestepped while simultaneously spinning. This freed my blade long enough to swing around to graze his back. He grunted and turned, furiously slicing at the air.

I took a few steps back while anticipating moves that might lead to his destruction. I flashed through the facts in my head—he was much larger, his strength was unmatchable, his reach was long, and he was quick with force.

I remembered my pendant in my pocket. If I could counter his attack long enough, I could jab my dagger through his side. Two weapons, after all, were better than one.

The pressure from another heavy blow almost sent me to my knees, but I somehow willed enough energy into my arms to keep from falling.

Sliding the pendant from my pocket, I felt it become warm as it extended into its dagger form. I held it tightly in my left hand as I fought with the sword in my right.

My strength was failing fast; it was time to make my move.

This time when he pushed his blade hard against mine, he leaned into it, positioning his body closer, and making himself vulnerable. *Now! Do it now!* instructed my voice of survival. *Never hesitate.*

With my lingering power, I pressed all my weight into my sword, and then swung the dagger into the space between. The dagger sank into his flesh, weakening his force. I shoved his sword from mine and sent his own blade into his neck. Blood shot from the puncture as he crumbled to the floor.

"You saved my life," said a grateful voice from behind.

I turned to the injured soldier. When I moved to help him from the debris, I realized how young he had been—barely sixteen, if I had to guess.

"I only did what needed to be done. Besides, we're in this together."

With his arm looped around my shoulder, I was able to move him away from the heart of all the fighting. As I propped him against the wall, I noticed a shrouded figure wearing a bronze battle helmet, dart to the fallen I had slain, pulling the dagger from the body. I couldn't believe I'd forgotten it.

"Hey you, stop!" It seemed such an odd thing to shout, with everything going on, but it was my first reaction. Without so much as a pause, the figure took off with my dagger and disappeared into the ongoing chaos of the room. I continued to push forward, searching in the direction he'd gone. Where was he going?

I looked back to the injured soldier, resting quietly where I'd laid him. His wound was a wide slash across his chest, a nasty injury, but not a fatal one.

"Go, I'll be alright," he shouted, as if he could read my thoughts.

I nodded, before moving forward. I'd already lost the blade of Tiger Lily, I wasn't about to lose the dagger, too.

I caught a glimpse of the dagger, a small glow from across the hall. The hooded figure still held it in his hand as he darted through a high archway.

I fought my way around everyone, slashing at the enemy, pushing everyone out of my way. It was a miracle that I was able to get through the arena in such good time.

Once I made it to the arch, I followed the sound of clinging chainmail down the course of the passage, out a courtyard, past an enormous fountain of an eagle, into the doorway of a tower. I paused when I reached a great spiraling flight of broken steps to catch my breath. The sound of the hooded thief's escape echoed down from the tower, teasing me as I looked up into its high rise. Gulping one last breath, I charged after the sound.

Every turn I would catch a glimpse of his cloak darting around the spiral curl, just outside of my reach. I shouted several times for him to stop, but he continued to run. I chased after him, winding around the crumbling stairs that climbed up the stone cylinder, until the stairs ended.

On each side of the landing were two rounded doors, one to my left and the other to my right. The tower railing had been so covered with soot that a smudge was left on the door that the figure had used to escape—the right door.

I drew my sword, readying myself for any possible attack.

My hands gripped the hilt hard while I pulled on the door's iron handle. I was careful when it opened, paying close attention to the new surroundings.

A smoky wind blew at my face, sweeping the ashy ruins of the island even this high above the land. The entire kingdom was visible from here, including the ocean around it. My feet moved on to a narrow platform. The platform seemed to stretch almost forty yards from the tower before ending in another one. I was standing at the top of the very outer walls of the castle.

The cloaked man ran down the length of the wall, stopping just before he reached the second tower, waiting. I ran after him, slowing as I closed the yards between us.

"Give me back the dagger," I yelled. The bronze helmet that covered his entire head did not move as he continued to stare out over the wall. He appeared to be waiting for something.

I cleared my throat and repeated my demand. "Hand over the dagger, and I'll bring you no harm," I promised. "All I want is the dagger."

He remained very still, making it quite clear that he was not planning on responding to my demands.

As I advanced to him, I noticed that the wall was very fragile, with bulging stones and holes that fell straight through. Each step sent pebbles of the stone bouncing down the side of the walls, landing in a wide gorge below us. I assumed the gorge held water at one time, possibly served as an entryway to expected visitors, but now it was merely a dry cracked canyon—a death trap if anyone were to fall over the edge.

A thin drawbridge, swayed over the gorge, hanging from only two of its four original chains. With each gust of wind, I could hear its chains rattle and boards creak. It was oddly quiet on the long platform, except for those rattles and creaks.

Even as I neared, the man in front of me did not move.

Let's see if he reacts differently at the tip of my blade, I thought.

"The dagger," I repeated, stretching my sword in a threatening manner. "Give it to me." I stood only a few steps away now.

In a split second, his cloak moved, bringing the movement of his sword with it. Steel met steel.

The initial strike sent pain shooting up my unprepared wrist, instantly weakening my strength. I stepped back to regrip my hilt, clenching it with both hands instead of one. He was strong, stronger than any opponent I'd ever fought.

His blade wasted no time, slashing fast at my head. I dipped down just in time to miss its strike. I countered quickly as he repositioned. Step, lunge, step, lunge. Using the strongest part of my sword, I struck the end of his, deflecting his blade. This parry put me close enough to attack. I lashed at his fighting arm, drawing the first blood.

I swung my blade for a second attack, but this time he countered, crossing his blade to mine. His moves became very quick, staying slightly ahead of mine. Two steps forward, lunge, one step back, counter. My opponent was coming at me fast and strong. Skillfully charging with more force than I'd ever encountered. He quickly gained ground, pushing me further and further back to the tower behind me. He seemed to know my every move, even before

I knew myself. Could he read my mind? I'd lost fifteen yards in a matter of minutes, and I was losing more ground. Had I met my match? Was this cloaked man going to be the end of me?

Soon his blade caught and spun around mine, maintaining contact until the force of motion knocked the hilt from my hand. My sword flew into the air, landing yards behind me. Without a weapon, I was completely in his control.

I tripped, landing on my side, as I scrambled to retrieve my weapon. I crawled as fast as I had the energy to, then reached for my sword. As my fingers neared the steel of my blade, the man hovered silently over me, placing his sword in position for the final strike.

I looked up at the figure above me and froze to brace for the strike. His helmet tilted as he stared down the length of his sword. This was it. There was nothing but sound now—his cloak whipping in the gusts of wind, the chains of the drawbridge rattling below us, loose pebbles bouncing their way down the side of the wall. Then I heard another sound coming from behind, an indistinguishable sound—a sound that distracted my enemy.

In seconds a short sword flew over me, driving deep into my attacker's thigh. Blood dripped from his wound as he limped back and wrenched the blade out of his leg.

I glanced over my shoulder to see Edmund charge from the tower. He moved swiftly, skirting around me and leaping over the space that stood between him and my enemy. The black gloves on his hands were stretched taut, gripping a second weapon held at a forty-five-degree angle. He was ready to kill.

The enemy had shuffled back, giving his full attention to Edmund.

Edmund swooped in fast, pushing the man further and further away from me. The injury to the enemy's leg put Edmund at a great advantage. With a wound that great on the right thigh, the cloaked man could only lunge on his left.

Edmund pounded the steal of his sword over and over on that weak right side, forcing his way to a winning position. Sparks erupted from the two steel blades as they clashed with each angry attack. Edmund never let up. He kept lunging and attacking the enemy's weak side. The hilt of his sword smashed into the metal of the enemy's mask, expelling the helmet from his head, revealing his true identity.

I had prepared myself for a lot of things. Seen a lot of things. Expected a lot of things. But one thing that I hadn't seen, hadn't expected, hadn't prepared for was the very thing I was faced with now.

His face was much thinner than I remembered, his eyes coated with a film of darkness and sunken below his brow, but I knew him.

"Father?"

Through that dark facade, it was his eyes that I still recognized. Eyes that a daughter could never forget. Why had he fought me? *Does he not recognize his own daughter? He should have run to me as soon as he saw me. He should be holding me now. He should be telling me how much he's missed me. How much he loves me...*

"Father," I cried, this time with certainty.

He looked away, keeping his eyes fixated on the deep rocky canyon below.

Edmund's blade rose to strike, a strike that would send my father to his death. The man who stood quiet and still looked hardly like the man who raised me, but he was still my father. He was behind those dark eyes, somewhere trapped inside his own body. He had to be.

"No!" I screamed. I dashed in front of Edmund, using my sword and body to protect the man I still called father.

"Move," Edmund demanded

"I won't let you kill him."

"Clara, he tried to kill you!"

"But he's still my father."

I turned to face him just in time to glimpse a softness return to my father's eyes, and then just as quickly, his eyes turned slate dark—blank and cold. Something had a hold of him, something deep, something dark. He was trying to fight it, but the darkness was winning.

When his eyes turned against me, so did he. My father pushed me forward into Edmund. I collapsed, bringing Edmund down with me.

He stood at the ledge for a single moment, looking at us heaped together, struggling to get back up. And then he leaped from the wall.

I screamed automatically, an impulse that barely expressed the horror I felt. I dashed to the ledge, afraid to see what had happened, but knowing that I had to look. That was when I saw it.

The black creature—the dark-winged Friesian we had met before—swooped below, catching my father with ease. Its wings moved quickly, as did its lean legs. The Friesian neighed and snorted, a sound that echoed between the canyon walls as it flew away with my father, following the streak of smoke left by Erik's blazing stallion.

I crumbled down into the stone, releasing the first of what I knew would be many tears. *How could my father do this? Why?* I found myself unable to speak, hardly able to breathe as the sobs took hold. *My father can't be bad…he can't be the enemy…*

"Clara, are you injured? Clara?"

Someone's voice buzzed in my ear. Edmund's.

Only minutes had passed, but those horrible minutes felt like hours of horror. I could hear Edmund's voice in the background, but I couldn't make sense of it over the questions rattling in my mind.

"Clara, please…talk to me," he pleaded.

His hands were wrapped around my shoulders now, gently shaking me back to awareness. My eyes looked away from the place where my father had stood only minutes before.

"How could he?" I asked, unaware that it was aloud.

Edmund wrapped his hand around my head, guiding it to rest against his chest. I could hear his heartbeat gently pounding in a slow rhythm. His voice overlaid the steady beat.

"It's not his fault, Clara. He doesn't know what he fights for—his mind is captive, his perception has been tainted."

I found myself drying my eyes with the back of my hand.

"Did you know about this? That he fought for them?"

"I only knew that he had been captured."

I buried my face into his shirt, trying to forget the dark image of my father.

"It's not his fault," he repeated.

It wasn't his fault. Did he believe that? Or did he say it because it's what I needed to hear? I wanted so badly to believe him, and for my sanity's sake, I needed to. But was it true?

As he rocked me back and forth, I felt strangely comforted and close to him. Edmund had escaped from the darkness. He had pulled away. He was the only person that knew what any of that was like. Could my father do the same? Could my father change, just as Edmund had?

I noticed that Edmund's expression was torn as his gaze fell to the courtyard below us.

There were voices, ringing out. It wouldn't be much longer before they discovered our location.

At this point I didn't care if they arrested me. My world had already been turned upside down. If the dark side had been able to get to my father, to turn him against his own beliefs—his own daughter—then what hope was there for me? But I didn't want Edmund to face trial; it would be certain death for him. A cruel, useless death at the hands of my own people.

"Edmund, you must go," I said. "They're coming."

"I will not leave. Not without you."

I blinked away tears to look up into his eyes. They were soft now, warm gentle swirls of brown. All the darkness had melted away. I had trouble looking into their warmth; a fast glance into them was enough to make me feel things that I shouldn't. Their richness pulled at my heart. Looking into them had become my guilty pleasure.

"If I go with you, they will hunt us both down. I need you to go alone. I need you to survive, for me."

"If your feelings are that of before...if they have not changed..." He paused. "If you care nothing for me still—please, tell me. Silence the hope that burns inside me."

I couldn't bring myself to say the words, to admit the truth, but I loved him. It was a different kind of love, not as brilliant and deep as my love for Finn, but it was still love. *Is it wrong for me to feel this way? If every person is born with two sides, one good, one bad, is it possible that each side could love a different heart?*

I slowly raised my hand, hoping that I would think of the right way to respond before my fingers reached his mask. The back of my hand caressed the stiff curve of the mask's cheekbone while his fingers made their way to touch my lips.

"You have a place in my heart," I whispered. "I think you always have, I was just too stubborn to see it."

Hesitantly, I brought my hand to the corner of his mask, hoping to pull it away. The distant picture of his face in the glow of the moon still lingered in my mind, but I wanted to look upon his face freely, with no mask or distance of any kind between us. I wanted to fully see the man who risked his soul for me so that I might understand a fraction more of him.

Before I could lift it away, his hand slid over mine.

"It is best if you do not see what lies beneath," he whispered. "Remember the face of the innocent boy, the face before all of this."

"You don't need to hide anymore. You're nothing like them, not at all. I have seen the good in you. Please, let me see you. Let me touch your face. Even if it's only this once."

His eyes showed gratitude for my words.

"There will be a time when you are meant to see me. I promise you that," he said. "But you must promise me one thing first."

"Okay."

"Promise to look at me as if you love me, as I love you. Promise to look at me the way you look at him."

Him. Hearing Edmund talk of my love for Finn tore at me. I wanted to try to explain, but I knew there was nothing to say. Edmund already knew the truth. I gently nodded my head in a silent agreement.

"If you love me, then you will run," I whispered. "Don't let them find you."

His eyes flashed down to meet mine. He slowly released my hand from his to cradle the back of my neck. I froze from his cool touch, unable to comprehend the thoughts rushing into my mind. The same hands that had once threatened me now held me protectively. I didn't understand him, and a part of me believed I never would. I felt myself pulling toward him and away, almost simultaneously. My two sides, my two feelings were at war—fighting against each other in my mind.

He leaned in, and a soft coolness touched my forehead. With that kiss he gently released my neck from his hands.

"So strange, yet perfectly beautiful," he said.

Those were his last words to me.

The voice of the guard reverberated from the courtyard, breaking our gaze.

He was gone in almost an instant, darting down into the tower. I saw the movement of his silhouette across the outer wall, stopping a moment to take one last glance back at me. He disappeared after that. A tingle lingered on my skin for a few moments after, before all traces of him were completely gone.

I loved them both. They were mortal enemies, but they shared something eerily in common. They shared a place in my heart. Two passions, so eagerly ripping me apart.

17

TEARS FALL

I HADN'T MOVED WHEN THE GUARDS ARRIVED. THE ARMY followed, flooding from the two towers like ants from an anthill. The three members of the guard that had made it through the battle remained close as if they were afraid I might plan an escape.

I remained seated with my arms folded closely to my body. I had no desire to move, much less run. I heard the guards talking around me. Something about they'd witnessed the whole affair. There was no need to hear it all, I knew what they meant. It was clear what they saw—me helping the enemy, again. I would be under arrest soon; there was no doubt about that. *I guess it won't be long before everyone knows about my father.* I grimaced.

Finn pushed through the men, ordering them to back off. That was really all I heard before he dropped to his knees.

"Clara, the battle is over. We have taken back the castle. The kingdom belongs to the Zyons once more."

The battle was won. We had reclaimed the kingdom of Zy and its people, but I still felt as though I'd lost. Everything had changed now. My father fought against me—and if I managed to stay alive, he would undoubtedly fight me again. Edmund was gone. And Finn would be out of my reach soon.

Not that he'd ever been within my grasp. The guards would surely deliver me to the kingdom of Everest in chains, where I would face the judgment of the Senate. And then there was the prophecy and the future of this world if Erik was not stopped—if I wasn't kept from his reach. How was I to cope with all of this when I'd lost everything? Including the blade of Tiger Lily and the cross pendant that had protected me so many times before. Yes, the battle was won, but just in time to start a war. The war of all ages.

"This is only the beginning," I murmured. "Erik was right. They will come again and they will be much stronger. They will come for me."

"We will be prepared when they do. I promise you. He will not get what he wants." He placed his hand on top of mine, smiling briefly to reassure me of his promise. "Today, we must be thankful for the battle we have won, the lives we have saved."

The sun rose above the ocean from far away, touching the lagoon in which we had anchored. All of the men, women, and children gathered behind the wall in the courtyard and all along the tops of the outer walls, watching it rise slowly above the island. The cold and bitter landscape was touched with the pastel colors of the sun. And through it all came a soft, cheerful melody—the song of the Zyon people. None of us outsiders understood a single word, but it was the most powerful melody my ears had ever heard. It resonated far beyond the walls of the castle, whispering over the entire land.

I felt something powerful in my chest—a mixture of feelings that I couldn't quite sort. We had won the battle but prompted a war—and I was fighting for one side, while my father stood to fight for the other. The feeling of victory seemed to be trumped by a fusion of pain and burden.

The onlookers parted, allowing Kalani to cross into the bubble around us. Today the princess of Zy had reclaimed her land, her people. Today a princess had become a queen.

Kalani moved closer, kneeling so that all three of us were in a row, looking out on the land of her kingdom. Tears rolled down her face, turning to gold as they dropped from her skin. I knew her heart was aching, just as mine, for a similar reason. She had won her kingdom back, but she had still lost so much.

Her lips parted, whispering the same native song that her people sang. It was then that I somehow began to understand it. They sang of love and hope for their future. They sang for the ones lost and the ones saved—they sang for tomorrow.

Their song signified that they would rise again—they would make it through the night and wake to a beautiful morning. Even through their loss, the Zyons had somehow found hope.

As my tears sprinkled the grey rock of the re-claimed castle's wall, I could only pray that I would live long enough to find the hope I'd lost—the hope I'd thrown away into a soulless sea.

Finn's warm hand gently touched my shoulder.

I didn't have to turn to see his face; I already saw it so clearly in my mind. I knew him. The way he moved and spoke. Every single smile for every single occasion, every last fault of his equaled perfection, I knew it. There was not a moment of my life that I didn't remember him. Of course, my love for him had changed—evolving over the course of time like a seed developing to its full potential.

He had been so much to me. A friend, a confidant, my love. To have someone so close to you and one day see that person in a completely different light—to see and love that person in an entirely different way. To hold a desire, a want and need for him and to know that it could never be. Forbidden. I could never have more than what I had now. And what I had was nothing more than a dream.

They both were forbidden. It was my curse, an unending punishment, and a waste of my heart. Finn and Edmund were a part of me, running through my bloodstream like sweet adrenaline, keeping me alive. All of our past, present, and future intertwined like an ever-growing grapevine, but why? I knew that I needed them both, just as much as they needed me. I just didn't understand. Why did I feel such a strong connection with them? How can you love two hearts, when you only have one?

By the end of it all, did my love even matter? I was faced with a trial where I would surely be found guilty of a crime. Punished, sentenced to death, unless the Senate had mercy. It would be for the best, more than likely, because if I lived through it, I would be faced with another challenge—a challenge I didn't believe I could win.

The war was on its way. And it was only a matter of time before Erik would come for me.

-18-

IMPRISONED

IT TOOK FIVE DAYS TO JOURNEY BACK TO EVEREST. THIS TIME, it was a completely different journey. I was guarded more intensely. I was kept away from the others, away from Finn. The three guards that remained alive knew that if they did not return to the Senate with me in chains, they would be held accountable for my escape. That was how our law worked. To an outsider, it might seem strict, but the laws of Everest had always kept order within our country. Our laws gave us a foundation that many of our allies envied.

I had decided to go willingly, leaving my fate to a man that I loved and the handful of senators who represented our country. This was how it had to be; there was no need to fight it.

The closer we came to the castle of Everest, the lower my spirits became. Each day I took in every piece of the world, knowing that it might be my last chance to see any of it. The soft green grass under my tired feet, the tall trees twinkling with their pine light, the birds that jetted by over our heads, the soft wind that curled my hair, the sun that filtered down to warm my skin—I memorized it all.

The day we came upon our village, which lay nestled against the towering outer walls of the castle, was too soon. I kept my head held high, momentarily forgetting my impending fate to admire the reconstruction of each building and household. Our entire kingdom had been renewed since my last journey through it. No more ghostly streets, no more eerie shadows, or ash. No more gloom or emptiness that had been left by the renegade. The streets were bright and alive with people again. I heard the pleasant sound of children playing and a steady tap coming from the blacksmith's shop as we entered. Mothers and their children ran through the streets to greet the soldiers with joy-filled hugs and laughter. There were a few glances my way, but most eyes stayed fixated on the returning soldiers. I was glad of this.

After passing through the crowds that had gathered in the streets of Everest, we came to the courtyard of the castle. The courtyard was beautiful, filled with the sweet smells of yellow roses and hibiscus, and groomed bushes that circled a brilliant fountain. It looked very similar to the illusion that Edmund had once created. The brilliancy carried on inside the castle walls. Each hall had been gutted of all the broken and burned items from before, replaced with new furniture, new paintings, and new coats of armor. There was no more smell of smoke in the castle, only clean herb smells that filled every space. Elaborate carvings decorated the stone columns that had once been covered in vines and soot. The open ceiling beams were now edged in gold and silver. The torn drapes were replaced with dark royal blue ones that moved with the slight breeze that blew down each hall. The entire castle had transformed into the grand place I remembered as a child.

I was escorted by the same three guards down the only hall that led to the prison cell, tucked underneath the castle. Finn had convinced them to remove my chains, but two of the guards were sure to keep a firm grip on each of my arms.

We finally came to the stairs that dropped down into the bottom of the castle. The stairs turned as we walked further down, ending in a dark narrow room that smelled of rust. There was only one window down here, a long narrow one that seemed to be squished into the top of the wall. One torch lit the entire room, and it rested on the wall, hanging above a wooden desk. This was where the guard or guards, depending on how big of a threat they thought I was, would be sitting through the night. Apparently, there would be two.

A wall of thick iron bars formed several square cells to the right of the stairs. A prisoner, a frumpy middle-aged man, was curled up in the corner of the cell closest to the door, talking nonsense to himself. I couldn't help but wonder how long he'd been down here. Months, going by the look of his cell.

The four guards that escorted me down nodded to the two on duty, filling them in on my charges. I only halfway listened, still absorbed in my unbecoming environment.

The cells contained only a small stool to sit on, a wooden plank for a cot, and a bucket for a toilet. Oh, how I hoped I wouldn't have the need to use the bucket.

Before long I was looking out from behind the bars. I stood for a while, pacing the square outline of my cell, then finally took a seat on the straight plank of wood that would later serve as my bed. I pushed my back against the wall and pulled my legs up to my chest, trying to limit the parts of my body that touched anything in the confined space.

The next hour was filled with strange sounds coming from the half-crazed man in the cell next to mine and grunting from the guards as they arm-wrestled to pass the time. The arm wrestling led to rematch after rematch, until they finally tired of it and settled down to play a game that appeared similar to chess. They never spoke to me, which really came as no surprise. In their eyes, I was a sinister woman, a traitor to my own country, from what they'd been told.

It was in the third hour of my imprisonment that a familiar voice rose above all the others.

"Clara, are you alright?"

Before looking up, I knew that the voice belonged to Finn.

"They haven't hurt me, if that's what you want to know," I said.

"This isn't right," he said, keeping his voice low. "You shouldn't be down here. You shouldn't be on trial. I've tried to meet privately with the Senate, to inform them of your innocence, but they won't have it. The members of the guard have given their statement, that you helped Edmund escape—that you've been helping him all along. They told of your father's turn to evil, and they are convinced that you have turned as well."

Finn paused for a moment, wrapping his hands around the bars that stood between us.

233

"The Senate was led to believe you were scheming to break the union between Everest and Zy. They have called for a public trial, Clara. The Senate feels this is a matter that should involve the entire kingdom, that treason should be punished publicly," he said. "Tell me what I can do. Please tell me something, anything that will prove your innocence."

I stared at my knees, not rising from the bench. "I am prepared to take whatever punishment they see fit."

He growled in frustration. "The crimes they accuse you of are punishable by *death*. I will not let you do this."

I turned my back to him, staring down at a long dusty crack in the stone floor.

"Clara, say something. Please."

The hope and pleading in his voice finally cracked my resolve to hide my turmoil of feelings from him, to protect him from my real guilt. "What do you want me to say? That I wanted this?" My tone was harsh and filled with unwanted emotion. I got to my feet to face him. "I have no other choice. I never did. I wanted too much. That is my crime, Finn. That is the real reason I'm in here, behind these bars. I can't deny that I secretly wished against the merge of the two kingdoms—against you marrying Kalani. I can't. I can't lie and say that I didn't help Edmund escape. Or tell them that my father hasn't turned dark, that he isn't now the enemy. That I didn't help him, too."

The cell felt like it was shrinking around me, becoming smaller with each emotion I exposed to Finn. I had so desperately wanted there to be another way, but everything I felt, everything I admitted to, indicated that I deserved to be behind the bars.

"Don't you get it?" I finished, deflating. "This is where I belong."

"You are not a traitor," he said. "I am the one who is guilty of destroying the treaty with Zy. I am the one who should be held accountable."

"Make me hate you, please," I begged. "Make me hate you right now so that I can face them tomorrow. I can't feel like this anymore. If I can't have you, then I must hate you. There's no other way I can face this."

"I will not. I will stand beside you."

"Why are you doing this to me?"

"Because I—"

"Don't say it. Please. That will only kill me more certainly than the Senate."

"Then know that I belong to you. Every part of me is yours from this day to the end of days. I will always be yours."

One of the guards from behind cleared his throat, signaling our meeting was over. It almost came as a relief to me, knowing that I wouldn't have to bear the pain of looking at him any longer. The more I was near him, the more my heart ached. I loved him, but none of it mattered now. I would soon be facing a panel of elders—the Senate. And they would decide my fate. I had to come to terms with this. I had broken the law, but not by treason. No, it was love that had been my crime. And I would soon pay for it. The Senate would decide if I would live another day to love Finn. Or they would decide how I was to die. Either way I was doomed.

If they didn't kill me, then the aching in my heart would surely take my life.

JUDGEMENT DAY

Dawn came sooner than i expected, bringing me that much closer to my fate. The same three guards who had escorted me to my cell greeted me as soon as the narrow window in the prison began to glow with the soft light of the new day.

Their heavy boots clicked loudly as we made the long walk to the great hall. This would be the platform for my judgment day. I focused on the clicking to keep myself from going any further with that kind of thought. If I was going to appear calm, then I needed to refrain from thinking about the certain outcome of my future.

As we neared, a rush of voices echoed around us. There was a large audience, no doubt. We entered the hall on the bottom floor, eye level with the hundreds of faces pushing each other aside to get a good look at me. I couldn't figure out if I should hold my head high or keep my eyes on the floor. I settled on staring at someplace in between.

The great hall was so beautiful today. The rafters had been painted, and the mural of angels on the ceiling had been refreshed so that the colors were even more vivid. The tiles on the floor had been polished, and so had the tile on the spiral staircases. Everything shined. New blue tapestries had been added, and a matching carpet ran down the stairs of the platform that held the king and queen's thrones. Even the grand clock in the back of the room had been cleaned to flawlessness.

I was led to the center of the room and forced to stand on a makeshift platform constructed of two short crates. I guess they wanted to make sure that everyone could see me, which made me feel even more awkward.

Directly in front of me was Finn, sitting on his throne wearing a troubled expression. Seven senators stood divided on the two staircases at the front of the hall, wrapped tightly in their white cloaks that covered all but their faces. Each member had white hair and long facial hair. They looked more like wizards from a storybook than senators. Definitely not the elders I remembered from my childhood.

I took a couple of deep breaths as they stepped down from the staircases and came together on the steps below the throne. It was beginning.

The volume from the crowd lowered immediately, leaving the great hall in a vacuum of silence. Finn seemed to shift uneasily on his throne.

A deep voice rang out from a member of the Senate.

"Clarabella Calahan, you are charged with aiding and abetting the escape of Edmund William Drake and for conspiring against the union of Everest and Zy. What have you say to these charges?"

My hands became clammy as soon as I realized I would have to answer.

"My loyalty is to this kingdom and this kingdom alone. My actions were in just cause. If you find that to be a crime, then there is nothing I can do or say that will change your minds. I purposely set Edmund free, but he should have never been arrested," I said. "And as for the rest, I cannot say that I did not wish against the merge, but not because I did not want our kingdoms to remain allies. It was for an entirely different reason. A reason that I wish to remain undisclosed."

"So you admit to the charges, then?"

"I have accepted them."

"And you do not wish to defend yourself?"

"I have nothing more to say."

People in the crowd began to whisper among themselves. I felt their stares as their whispers burned my ears. My only wish was that my judgment would come quickly, but it seemed that time had stalled just to agitate my last nerve. What was taking so long? Why wouldn't they end this already? I told myself to keep breathing. That was all I could do now. *Just breathe.*

"So be it. Does anyone have anything to add before judgment is passed?"

"I do," Finn's voice seemed to fill the entire hall. He suddenly rose from his throne, standing tall and with a grace I could never imagine possessing. He stepped down each carpeted step of the platform, parting the group of senators. As he neared, I felt less and less alone on that podium of shame. And when his eyes met with mine, I had a sudden fear that he was about to put himself in harm's way to try to save me.

"What are you doing?" I whispered when he came to stand next to me. But I knew he wouldn't answer.

"Hear me, senators," he commanded. "I ask that you release Lady Clara immediately."

"You wish to set a traitor free? She has done a disservice to this kingdom. She must be punished."

"You have not seen what I've seen, senators. This woman that stands before you has shed blood fighting for this kingdom and is the very one responsible for Victor's downfall. She is a hero, a true guardian. You must see that she is key to winning this battle, that she alone will lead us into our victory. I will lay down my crown and all of my rights as your king to see that she survives your judgment. And if you believe me to be your rightful king, then you will also believe this." His voice was unwavering, loud and strong. "She has brought hope once more to this land. And more importantly, she has brought hope to me. I call upon the Senate once more to relinquish the charges brought against her and to release her from the chains in which she does not belong."

"True guardian? Ha! Her own father has turned to the dark ways! It was only a matter of time before she followed. We already have more than enough witnesses to place her in the company of those who brought about this war. The very ones who killed your family. What have you say to that, young king?"

"She was merely victim."

"That is not what we have heard. The members of the guard say that she helped one of the fallen escape. The man we know as Edmund. That doesn't sound like a victim. Your judgment is clouded, young king. Blinded by her beauty, no doubt."

"Then so be it. If you feel you need to pass judgment on her, then you must pass the same judgment on me."

I couldn't stay silent. "Finn, no. This is my punishment to bear, not yours!" I shouted, but my words were lost somewhere in the space between us.

"Now don't be hasty, sire. Why would we punish you for her crimes?"

"Because I'm guilty...I'm guilty of loving her."

The entire room gasped together, and then a hush rolled through the crowd.

Finn stood facing the court as the words left his mouth. He said it without a hint of doubt or regret in his voice, and then he turned his back to the Senate to face me with searching eyes.

"And that is a crime I would gladly commit every day for the rest of my days," he said. "Punish me how you will. I love her."

"You would place yourself on trial for the love of a woman? A traitor, no less? Do you hear yourself?"

"I hear and believe every word I've said, but I cannot do as the Senate has asked of me. I took an oath to God and my country that I would bring justice to all, protect those who could not protect themselves, to vanquish evil from our lands, and to bring freedom to our country. But how can I fight for a country that would banish the greatest of all liberties? What freedom do I fight for, if not the freedom to love? Senators of the court, I cannot serve as king to such a country."

"What are you suggesting, young king?" the senator spokesman asked, disbelief evident in his voice.

"This is no suggestion," he said. "I simply cannot marry another, even if it will unite our kingdoms. If this makes me a traitor to the crown, then so be it. Take the crown from me."

He set his crown on the floor in front of us and clasped my hand in his.

"You must bind me as you have bound her."

The faces of the senators twisted with confusion as they began to talk among themselves. The crowd around us roared with conversation. No one seemed to know what to think about what was just said, much less how it should be dealt with.

The minutes passed slowly, bringing the worst kind of anxiety with them. Finn stood beside me, with his body frozen tall and his head held high. He had gripped my hand in his, ignoring the chains that rattled from my wrists. He looked sure of himself and the decision he had made, but this was not a look I shared. My life was already on trial, but for him to throw his in with it was unbearable. If I had to die, I wanted to at least die knowing that he was free to live.

Finally, a senator's voice broke through the buzz of our audience.

"Quiet down! We have made our decision!"

Silence.

My grip tightened around his fingers until I couldn't feel my hands. I held my breath, waiting for their verdict. The room was hot. I didn't remember it being this hot before. My neck became dewy with perspiration; my fingers felt damp in Finn's hands. This was it.

A small voice rang through my mind, asking if I was ready. I fought the urge to say no. How could I ever have prepared myself for a moment like this? What started out as my fate had become the fate of us both—our fate. The sound of my heartbeat thumped in my ear, muting the clanging of the shaking chains.

The warm sensation from before became a burning. My feet suddenly went numb; my legs felt heavy, my stomach dropped as if someone punched my gut. A sharp pain shot through the tendons on my arm, drawing my fingers tighter around Finn's. My mouth became dry and my throat tightened without warning. It was becoming difficult to breathe. The room blurred out of focus. *What's happening to me?*

"Finn!" I winced in pain as he helped me from the podium.

I felt hundreds of eyes focusing on my face—a face that was twisting in pain, so I closed my eyes, trying to shut them out.

I forced my mind away from my current location, finding comfort in thoughts of Scarlet Heights. The cool breeze rustling roses in its courtyard. The lime green grass that covered the hills. The look of the moon shining on the swells of the ocean. I could almost picture it.

Then the pain got worse. Much, much worse.

I was sweating, but my body shook with chills, as if I had contracted a full fever in a matter of seconds. My toes curled when a sharp pain splintered through my feet. The same pain shot through my palms. It throbbed, pulsing with my heart, as it grew harsher and harsher. Then the pain began to spread, flowing through my tissues like a bad reaction to a drug. It pinched at every nerve and every muscle, starting at both ends of my body and joining forces at my abdomen. Nausea attacked my stomach as it twisted and turned from the pain. I moaned, trying my best to hold myself together.

My whole body began to feel as if it were being ripped apart, like a force pulled me in every direction. I opened my eyes to make sure my limbs were still connected, to make sure my organs weren't being torn from my body. To my surprise, everything was still attached. *What is this pain?*

Agony overcame me, knocking me to my knees. Had I been cursed? Was I dying? I heard a whimper escape my mouth, and it sounded so far away, as if it had come from another person entirely. Pressure was forced upon every organ in my body, and a louder cry erupted from me. My mind kept fighting against the pressure, the pain, the force, but the rest of my body had turned against me. The pounding of my heart hit harder against my chest, like a mallet against a tight bass drum. *Thud—thud, thud—thud—thud, thud.*

My body collapsed flat onto the floor.

I could feel Finn's fingers tighten around mine, his hand brush against my damp forehead. He was saying something to me, but my world was muted now. My body shook uncontrollably from the chill on my skin. Finn pulled me closer to him, giving me a split second of relief from the cold. I could see his eyes more clearly now, and they were filled with horror.

The harsh thud quickened, the number of beats grew too many to count. The pain pushed my mind away from this place, but it didn't know where to land. My thoughts looked for comfort. Familiarity. Finn's face was all I could see. The perfect lines and structure of his smile, the warmth in his green eyes. Green and warm like Ireland. I thought of home again. Only briefly, but I saw it perfectly. The deep blue ocean surrounding the rocky landscape of Ireland, the lime green colors of the lawn around the manor. The red roses of Scarlet Heights that never seemed to fade.

Then the world fell out from under me.

My body seemed to drop right through the floor of the castle, spinning into a colorful display of light. The great hall and Finn disappeared right before my eyes, turning into shades of blue, yellow, green, orange, pink, red. The colors streaked past me. Warmth overtook the chill on my skin, the cruel pain vanished, turning to a pleasant sensation, and I suddenly felt a thrill. I rode the wave of color as it pushed me further and further away. It was like riding a roller coaster on a sunny day, or holding your head out the window of a speeding car, but the wind was soft and comfortable, and I could see every particle of the colors so clearly.

In what felt like seconds, the ride slowed, and the colors began to merge together, forming shapes. A dark green tree flew past me, then a yellow flower, and a blue bird. More colors combined—more shapes.

I flew through a whole forest of trees and over a grassy field before I felt an incredible tiredness wrap my body like a thick blanket. Then, nothing. The ride was over. And I lay still in darkness.

-20-

THE GIFT

I THOUGHT I WAS PARALYZED.

No part of me would obey my instruction to move, not a single finger, a single toe, or even an eyelid. There was sound all around. A rustle of grass, water breaking, birds cooing, the buzz of an insect. I even heard my stomach rumble from hunger. I was trying to piece together what had happened.

Was it magic? A curse? I couldn't hear the commotion of the senators or the buzz of the crowd anymore. And I couldn't hear Finn.

My willpower finally broke the barricade that had paralyzed me. My eyes slowly adjusted to brightness. Clouds raced across their endless blue sky while the sun beamed high above them.

"Finn," I said as if to finish the calling from before. It fell from my lips, confirming I was able to talk again.

When my eyesight sharpened, revealing Scarlet Heights towering in the distance, it became clear what had happened to me. At least, it was the only logical explanation, as illogical as it might sound.

My gift had finally developed.

I had teleported.

I was a teleport.

So what did this mean? I had vanished from Everest, vanished before the senators—before they could pass my judgment. Had I left Finn? Was he now standing alone, trying to come up with an explanation for my disappearance? The Senate would chalk it up to magic, no doubt the evil kind. What would they do to my poor Finn? I had to go back somehow. I had to find my way back to him.

My hands were fists now as I tried to will feeling to my arms. I closed my eyes, squeezing them so tightly together that I saw stars. *Take me back. Please…please.*

I opened my eyes, looking to heaven as I begged. *Please, please.*

There was movement a few yards from me, a rustling in the long-stemmed wheat. I rolled over quickly and kicked my legs against the ground, trying to gain more feeling. They were still tingling like I'd been sitting with them crossed for too long. *Finn. Please, God. Please let him be with me.*

"Finn?" My voice was more hopeful this time.

The wheat shook again, and someone moaned. I crawled, pulling golden stems from the ground as I inched toward the movement and the sound. *It has to be him*, I thought. *It has to be.*

For the first time, his dark skin looked oddly pale, beaded with sweat and dirt. He was weak like me, his arms positioned oddly on the earth, but he was alive, and we were together. That was all that mattered now.

Finn.

I crawled next to him, laying my sore body back into the crinkled amber grass. His hand softly nudged the back of mine, inviting my fingers to curl into his. His eyes opened soon after, mesmerizing me as if it were the first time our gazes had ever met. My cheeks felt warm, as did my heart.

"Clarabella." His voice was so soft and sweet, lingering in the space between us. "Is this a dream?"

I nuzzled my head into the niche of his neck, rolling into a place that felt like home. "It feels like one," I said.

"Then I hope I dream forever."

I drew a much-needed breath, memorizing the tone in his voice and the brilliancy in his gaze. Neither one of us spoke. This was a moment that was ours and ours alone. No fear, no judgment, and no worry. As his lips warmed mine, pressing deeper and deeper into passion, everything came together. *Yes, this is how it should be,* I thought. *How it should always be.*

Just as the thought entered my mind, my eyes were lost to the bright blue above us, watching as the brilliant sun began to peep through shapes of fluffy white.

There was a part of me that felt guilty—a twist in my stomach that felt shame for the two opposing feelings that I knew were still trapped inside of me.

Two loves, one heart—each love forbidden in its own way. No apologies should be given for loving a man who had my heart, and for loving another who loved me with what was left of his. I had done what I had to do, and this was how it was—how it was meant to be. So why did I feel such guilt? Though my heart was slightly aching, I knew from the depths of my soul that it was Finn who I was destined to love. Yet, I still felt a confession was needed—an admittance of my guilt. It was burning in my throat like acid, waiting to be acknowledged.

My lips parted from Finn's as my mind raced with my feelings, with my guilt, with my words. I just couldn't bring myself to say it; I couldn't admit to what I was feeling, but it was there. It was there waiting...

I'm sorry, Edmund. Those were the words. *I'm sorry I couldn't be yours.*

Overhead, a familiar owl circled the sky.

ACKNOWLEDGEMENTS

It takes more than creativity and time to write a book. It takes the love and support of a lot of people. Here are my biggest supporters:

My husband, Clint Peery,
Who inspired me to dream and to write;

My parents, Cliff and Terry Eddy,
Who encourage me in all my endeavors, even the crazy ones;

My brother, Adam Eddy, and Nancy Diehl,
Who listen and cheer me on;

My extended family, Mike, Travis, and Sharon Peery,
Whose wanting to know what happened next, made writing it that much more fun;

My closest friend, Amy Isbell,
Who knows when I need to break from writing for girl time;

There have been so many more individuals who have given me essential feedback and encouragement along the way. If you're reading this, then you are a part of that support system, and you have my greatest appreciation. It's wonderful people like you that have made this possible.

JILLIAN PEERY is the author of the thrilling para-normal romance, *PineLight*. She currently lives in Texas with her husband, Clint, and mini-schnauzer, Zoe. To learn more about Jillian, visit her Web site at www.jillianpeery.com.